THE ONE

The Other Me

j. manoa

EPIC
Press

The Other Me
The One: Book #1

Written by J. Manoa

Copyright © 2016 by Abdo Consulting Group, Inc.

Published by EPIC Press™
PO Box 398166
Minneapolis, MN 55439

Printed in the United States of America.

Cover design by Candice Keimig
Images for cover art obtained from iStockPhoto.com
Edited by Ryan Hume

LIBRARY OF CONGRESS CATALOGING-IN-PUBLICATION DATA

Manoa, J.
The other me / J. Manoa.
p. cm. — (The one; #1)
Summary: Odin Lewis has always known he is different from everyone else: he can
levitate objects, look into the past, and learn things that no one else knows. Odin's
life changes when his old friend Wendell returns—trouble is, Wendell isn't real. Under his illusory friend's influence, Odin begins to question everything he thought he
knew about himself, his family, his friends, and his entire life, while slowly learning
more about his powers.
ISBN 978-1-68076-050-7 (hardcover)
1. Imaginary playmates—Fiction. 2. Interpersonal relations—Fiction. 3. Family
life—Fiction. 4. Psychic ability—Fiction. 5. Young adult fiction. I. Title.
[Fic]—dc23
2015949416

EPIC
Press

EPICPRESS.COM

To my dad, for his support throughout this series

1

CONSERVATION OF ENERGY—THAT ENERGY CANNOT BE created or destroyed—is the answer to question twenty-three on next Friday's exam. The same exam has been given to every junior physics class for the last twelve years.

"However, energy can be altered from one form to another," Mr. Zeller says. He motions with both his hands in front of him as though tossing an invisible tennis ball back and forth. "Like in a piece of dynamite. The chemicals inside hold potential energy." His hands stop moving. "This is then made into kinetic energy." He flips his arms up and out. "And we all know what that kind of energy does." He drops both hands and pushes off the desk behind him. "Watch any action movie from the last fifty years for that."

Mr. Zeller turns his back on our class to write on the board. Denise slides a folded paper onto my desk that reads, "For Erin." The paper is formed into a small rectangle, which unfolds when the tab on the front is pulled. All the girls in the class fold their notes like this. The note includes a rumor that Nicole, one of the girls who sits at the same lunch table with both Denise and Erin, was trying to get with Derek, one of the guys from the baseball team whom Erin also had a crush on. I tap Alex's desk to get his attention and slide the note under his arm as he furiously scribbles notes onto his paper.

I've never taken notes in this or any other class. My notes are a list of dates, the basic topic, and that night's homework. I typically use only one paper per class per week. I like doing my part to save the environment. Everything else, everything said in class or from the book, I already know or can picture. It's so easy that it almost feels like cheating, but it isn't. Not to me at least. It all comes from my head.

Mr. Zeller turns to us from the board on which he has drawn a box labeled 5 *kg*, a vertical line of 5 *m*, and the equation of potential energy: $m \times g \times h$ (mass times gravity times height).

"When the box hits the ground," he says, "the potential energy is zero." Question twenty-six: the kinetic energy equals approximately two hundred fifty joules rounded up.

He turns to the board again to write the equation for the rest of the class. I lean forward on my desk, elbows hiding my lack of notes, and glance over my shoulder, two rows back and three seats over.

Evelyn uses her purple pen for physics. She uses the same for trigonometry and what she considers the science classes. World Civilizations, Modern American Literature, and what she considers art classes are in green. Everything else, the miscellany which makes up a "well-rounded education," is blue. She has a red one as well but doesn't use it. It reminds her too much of her eighth grade English teacher who used a thick red marker to eviscerate students' work, until it looked shredded and bloody. She told me this.

She glances up at the board, her eyes as large and sweet as a puppy's. One look at her deep brown irises with gold streaks like flashes of light down a hallway and I forget that anything else exists in the world. At least for a moment, a moment that never lasts as long as I'd like. A couple of the guys think that her face is a little too round in the cheeks. David once said that she's like a squirrel and puffed his face out in imitation, but he was wrong. She glances to the side and I look away.

Next to the board is a big, color-coded poster of the periodic table of elements. There's still an impression and some ink left from where a senior named Leonard blacked out *Uranium* to add

Urassium with an atomic weight of *69*. None of the teachers who use this room found out who changed it. All the students know, not just me; it only took a couple of days to get out.

On the wall around the door is a flier for a school dance that happened two months ago. It's taped over a flier for a fundraiser from the beginning of the year. Next to the dance flier is an anti-drug poster that no one pays attention to anymore. Between the windows on the opposite wall are photographs of famous scientists: Albert Einstein, Marie Curie, Nicolaus Copernicus, Victor Scheffer, Galileo Galilei, with quotes under each of their faces. *Where the senses fail us, reason must step in.* That's Galileo's quote. Not, *And yet it moves,* which he never actually said.

Mr. Zeller walks around to the front of the desk and sits down on it. The lesson is done, but he always likes to spend the last few minutes sharing ideas that are never on the test. He has one minute left. The class is already packing their books. "Of course there are other theories about the creation and destruction of energy at an atomic level," he says.

Mr. Zeller was a lecturer at a university in Idaho fifteen years ago but was let go because of budget cuts in his department. The professor who decided to fire Mr. Zeller didn't even know that Mr. Zeller was having an affair with the professor's wife. So that's kinda funny, in a sad, poetic sort of way. I'm not sure if the professor ever learned of the affair or not. I can't picture the professor or his wife.

"Researchers have actually found that some electrons transfer from one location to another, or disappear completely, like teleportation." Mr. Zeller points at Miles in the fifth row, who he thinks is writing a note, but is actually finishing a drawing of a comic book character that he started during yesterday's class. "Don't worry, this won't be on the test." Most of the class has already put their books away and are watching for him to dismiss us. He thinks this means we're interested. "Some people believe this phenomena demonstrates a transference from one dimension to another, like the electron blinks out of one place, into another, and back." He's now two minutes over.

I did a presentation on a similar topic for last year's science fair. It was a mock-up of the Schrodinger's Cat experiment, except without the cat, radioactive material, or poison, mostly because Mr. and Mrs. Aukerman wouldn't let me borrow Whiskers, or whatever their cat's name is. From there the poster ventured into the "many worlds" interpretation, with one possible world being that the cat lived and the other being that the cat died. Which one we're living in, we'll never know, because there was no cat.

The project was inspired by something Wendell told me a long time ago: Of all the worlds in the universe, this is the only one where I was born. I mean, this version of myself. He said that makes me truly unique. But of course he would say that. We all want to imagine that we're unique.

"But that's all still very theoretical," Mr. Zeller says, "so don't expect to be teleporting to Paris anytime soon or anything." He waits for a laugh. It never comes. "Anyway, see you all tomorrow."

Most of the class rushes out the door while I'm still wedging my thick science text between calculus and Advanced Placement European history. Altogether my bag weighs just over twenty pounds, or nine kilograms. Sad to say I actually weighed it once. So at my height of sixty-seven inches, or approximately one point seven meters, I'm carrying almost one hundred fifty joules of potential energy with me for seven hours every weekday. And I'm not sure if the fact that I enjoyed doing that calculation in my head is encouraging or really depressing. I guess it depends on which world we're living in.

Evelyn is still talking with Maria in the hallway when I leave the classroom. Maria is always there, probably because our class is always late to get out. Evelyn's the taller of the two, but not by much, and also the prettier, by quite a bit. At least I think so. Richard thinks Maria is hotter because she has bigger tits, but I don't care. There's something about the way the tip of Evelyn's nose angles down to make it look like a diamond, or how her lips pull back when she smiles, as if she knows things that no one else in the world does . . . It's just so cute. I've always thought so, since before our first day of freshman year.

"Hey, Odin."

Shit. Maria caught me looking.

"Hey," I reply. "How's it going?"

She turns to Evelyn. "You ready?" Evelyn nods.

"See ya, Odin," Maria says as they turn to walk away. I can hear them laugh lightly as I move in the other direction. I begin to look back at them when someone else catches my eye. Kevin. With his dumbass spiky hair and t-shirts for bands he's never even listened to. I look down again and hope he ignores me as much as I wish I could ignore him.

I hear him mutter something as he passes.

It was, "Oddin."

It wasn't long into freshman year when Kevin stopped hanging out with me and spent more time with Dylan and Eric. It was okay, I mean, that's high school, right? Everyone changes. At least that's what my mom told me when I would mutter about Kevin not being my friend anymore. Mom said that high school is when we try to figure out who we really are. I shouldn't be too mad at him or feel too bad about losing someone who'd been my best friend throughout grade school. And I wasn't, after a while. He had his friends and I had mine.

Until sophomore year.

It was one of those days when both of my parents had meetings so I had two hours to kill before getting my ride home. They didn't allow me to catch the bus on my own then. I sat under the hoop of the school's basketball court reading *Of Mice and Men* when Kevin, Dylan, Adam, and Eric seemed to appear out of nowhere. I tried to look like I didn't notice them and focused on my book.

"What's up, Oddin?" Kevin said. It was the first time he'd called me that.

I didn't say anything and stared at the words that were suddenly invisible on the page.

"Weird," he said, stepping closer with his entire group.

Again, I said nothing. Four of them, each one bigger than me. Not much I could do. Not at that time.

"Still talking to your imaginary friend?" Dylan and Eric laughed.

"What?" I asked, foolishly allowing my attention to shift from the book to him.

"Yeah," he said, looking at his cronies. "This kid was so fucking pathetic in grade school that he actually had to imagine that he had a friend. Fucking loser." He turned to me and leaned in closer. "Isn't that right, Oddin?"

"No," I lied.

"Are you saying I'm lying?"

I put the book down. "I know you're lying." That one wasn't a lie.

"Oooooh," said Eric.

"You gonna let this little cocksucker say that?" said Dylan.

"Fuck you, Oddin," Kevin said, kicking my bag over in front of me. I stood up. "What you gonna do, you little shit?"

I pictured smashing Kevin's head into the metal posts holding up the basketball hoop and then tossing his husk off to midcourt like a soiled rag. Then I remembered my dad telling me about the need to control myself. Control is strength, he said. Bad things happen when you lose control.

That was when the first punch came. Down. Across my head. Like a brick. I didn't see stars. I didn't see anything. Just blurs. The next one was on my ear. Then right above my eye. I fell to my hands and knees and watched my blood drip in time with their hyena laughs.

"Oddin," Kevin said. "Little shit."

I told my parents that I'd accidentally been elbowed while playing basketball that afternoon. I added that there was always a game and maybe they could pick me up late every day so I could play a bit more. That was when they decided it would be best if I took the bus home immediately after school every day instead of waiting for them. They proposed it like it was their idea, exactly as I had hoped they would.

I hit my locker to lose some weight from my bag before heading to lunch. The line already stretches from the lunchroom out into the far end of the hallway, around one of the staircases to the second floor and beyond the intersection between most of the classrooms and the administrative offices. The path between them leads to the side exit for the basketball court and the auditorium. We're not supposed to use that exit.

I keep my locker open to block one side and check the other for anyone who could see me. Almost everyone who isn't in the lunch line is outside, all the way on the opposite end of the building, sitting at the senior or junior benches, or lining the walls near the front. I guess they just like knowing that there's a world outside of school, even if they can't enjoy it yet. I angle my back toward them.

I hold my pen flat in my open palm in front of me. I stare at the pen, a thin, semi-transparent cylinder with a plastic clip and a top button that has the most satisfying click whenever it's opened or closed. I admire the shadow the pen makes as it floats an inch above my hand.

2

"**N**O, NO, NO, THE BEST THING IS WHEN YOU SNEAK up from behind and slash a guy's throat with your knife," David says, mimicking the throat-cutting motion with his plastic fork. "Then, the idiot's in the chat like, 'I didn't even see that guy!'" I can see little bits of meat from the spaghetti sauce pop out of his mouth in excitement. They contrast badly against the piss-yellow lunch table top.

It was David who first suggested we make this our regular spot: first seats on the third table from the front and one from the right. Several tables away from the jerks we don't like—Kevin and Eric and them—and with a good view of both the swim team and Drama Club girls.

"Headshot is still better," Brent replies, returning to his usual premise. "Always headshots. From nowhere and boom! Total badass."

The funny thing about this room is how regimented it is. We already have assigned seats in most classes and claimed seats in others, so you'd think that we'd enjoy this period of freedom to at least move around. Perhaps the bits of paint hanging off the back wall of the cafeteria aren't so bad from the front, left corner, or maybe the eighth row back has a view through the large windows into the teachers' parking lot, so we can tell which ones are smokers. It would be a longer trip to the boys' room from there but at least moving around would mean having something other than the same old view every single day. Not that I mind seeing the swim team and the Drama Club girls, but perhaps even this view is better from somewhere else. Instead of trying out new possibilities, we assign ourselves to one place and remain there for the rest of the year, even if we no longer care for the company. I guess we've been conditioned well.

"Too impersonal," David says. "A real gamer likes to get his hands dirty."

"Dirty with what?" Richard asks with his usual skepticism.

"The blood of his foes."

"What blood?" Richard scoffs.

It's not even like a group or clique thing really. Brent and David could be near the back with Evan and the rest of the gamers, but they also played baseball last year which means they could sit alongside Derek and their other teammates. Richard plays online with them sometimes but also runs track and occasionally smokes weed with the stoners behind the bushes on the side of the school. Brent does as well. So that's three possible tables for both of them.

As for me, Mom and Dad made a big push for me to join the Debate team freshman year. They said it would be a nice mental exercise in considering the merits of each side of an argument. None of the other teammates listened to me, though, because I was the newcomer. When I finally got the chance to contribute last year, I could too easily know every word of the other team's argument. I wouldn't even have to prepare anything. I'd just focus for a moment and counter. It was like taking notes for a class or studying for a test. That information was my own, from my memory, stuff that I would ideally know anyway. Opponent arguments were not things I was supposed to know beforehand. At least not every word of them.

That group was lame anyway. A bunch of argumentative show-offs who always needed to fact check any little statement, even when it's being quoted directly, or who couldn't allow an opinion to be said without trying to change it. Resolved: Knife kills are more badass than headshots. Counterargument?

What I really wanted to do was play football, but

my parents absolutely refused to let me. For a week Dad was sliding print-outs under my bedroom door about the impact of concussions on high school players. He liked to say that my brain was too important to risk for any sport. Then he'd add, "As Socrates said, 'I think therefore I am.'" It was Rene Descartes who said that. Pretty sure he made the mistake on purpose but I never can tell with him.

I joined bowling instead. Got Brent and Richard and a couple other guys to come along. It's the only sport where you can have a burger, fries, and a drink during a game and the coaches don't mind. Also less chance of being hurt, other than the time Brent got his hand crushed by reaching for his ball right when Lucas pushed them all back. I imagine it's better than a concussion.

"Headshots take actual skill," Brent says.

"So does sneaking. The throat slash is just like a reward."

"There's no achievement for a hundred automatic knife attacks."

"There is for fifty."

"'Cause after fifty even the games get sick of it!"

Evelyn's laugh is like a Pavlovian bell. It's high and melodic, and it makes me turn every time I hear it. She sits at the end of the first table with Maria, Alison, Lori, Stephanie, all the other Drama Club girls. She also runs cross country, so that's at least two tables for her. It's a good combination: the lean build of a runner with the poise and presence of an actress. A bit intimidating in fact. Probably more than I'd admit.

Every year the school holds two productions. One of these is usually a modern piece chosen by the theatre teacher, Mrs. Bourne. Last year it was something about maids in the South during the Civil War. I don't remember the title and don't care enough to find it. Evelyn played the husband of the lead actress because there weren't enough boys for the male parts. She was good, despite having only fourteen lines that she had to deliver in this ridiculously low voice. She also had to wear a suit with tails and a top hat. She was tomboyish but still really cute, like a gem that no one else recognizes.

The other play was always Shakespeare. Always. Mrs. Bourne said it was because Shakespearean plays are the greatest in history and that being unfamiliar with Shakespeare means being unfamiliar with all of art, but it was actually because there's no copyright on the plays and no fees to produce them. The plays are on a four-year rotation. In freshman year Evelyn had one scene as Macduff's wife in *Macbeth*. Sophomore year she was Hortensio in drag for *Taming of the Shrew*. This year she was Lady Capulet in *Romeo and Juliet*. She joked about being upset that she had yet to die on stage.

The lead actress for either play is always a senior, even if a junior or underclass girl is better. That's what Maria told Evelyn after Judi Conners got the part of Juliet. No one knows which play will run in the fall but next spring is *Hamlet*. Evelyn is already memorizing lines for her Ophelia audition.

Act IV, scene v, Ophelia's madness. She's between a raving, schizophrenic performance and a giddier, more whimsical one. She's refused to watch any movie or theatre productions of the play. She says she doesn't want any other actress impacting her take on the part. However, she did watch a couple of YouTube clips two weeks ago. She told me this.

I try not to check on her. It makes me uncomfortable, like I'm a stalker, or a voyeur, or something generally creepy. Plus, truth is, I'm not sure how much I want to know.

"Man, how obsessed are you?" Richard's voice is distant and takes a moment to identify as directed at me.

"What?" I say.

"Always staring at Evelyn," he says.

"He's memorizing so he can fap to her later," Davis says.

"Shut up."

"Every day, as soon as he gets home."

"It's not—"

David half-shuts his eyes and opens his mouth to breath heavily. He makes a jerking off motion under the table. I look down trying to appear more angry than embarrassed. I see my fork starting to lift from the piss-yellow table. I press the fork down.

"Dude," Brent says, across the table from me, "it's been three years already, make a move."

I don't reply.

"Don't be such a wuss," David says.

I don't know why I still hang out with David.

Richard looks across the table. "Oh, c'mon," he says to David, "I heard you trying to ask Amanda out."

"For real?" Brent says. He laughs, tilting his head back. It's only when he leans back like that when it becomes clear that his right nostril is bigger than the left.

Richard continues in a meek voice, "Umm . . . uhh . . . I was . . . ummm . . . like, thinking that, uhh . . . maybe if you, like . . . I think maybe—"

Brent laughs again, louder.

"That's not what happened."

"I dunno," says Brent, "that's what she told me it sounded like."

Richard continues, "So like . . . umm . . . maybe if you . . . uhhh—"

"She's a bitch anyway."

"Only 'cause she turned you down," Richard says.

"I turned her down."

"No," Brent says, shaking his head. "You didn't. Everyone knows you didn't."

All the girls at the drama table are listening very closely to Alison. Her palms are flat on the table as she's bent low over it. Looks like something interesting, but probably not worth knowing. Or not violating trust in order to know. If it's important, I'll find out from Evelyn or from the general flow of information through the rest of the student body. The best way is always from that person, Evelyn or whoever it is. That way it becomes their choice to tell. They want me to know. Me and no one else.

Besides, like Dad used to say all the time, there's a reason people keep certain things private. They don't want to hurt us.

The conversation at the Drama Club girls' table continues as Kevin walks past with his empty lunch tray. He stops and leans in to listen. He looms over them like the predator he is, staring through the huge, fake nerd glasses that dumb people think make them look smart and stylish. He looks over each of them one by one, Evelyn last.

"That guy is such a dick," Brent says, his eyes paralleling my own.

David glances to see who it is. "He's not that bad," he says. "Gave me a lift home one time."

"He has a car?" Richard asks.

"Yeah, big one too. His parents gave it to him for his sixteenth birthday. Before he even got his license."

Kevin told me about that arrangement years

ago. Back when we were friends. He gives a horse-faced smile as he stands and walks away from the group. The girls continue on without concern.

"Have you invited her to your party?" Brent asks.

"Yeah. She said she'll come but wants to bring Maria along with her."

"Tell her to make Maria wear a really tight shirt," Richard says.

"She can do that when it's *your* birthday," I say. "She texted me last week that she'll be there."

"I thought you don't get texts," David says.

"I do." *Just not from you*, I want to say. "But only for really important things. My parents don't like me using it."

"Texts from Evelyn are 'really important things'?" asks Richard, ever the skeptic. He would fit in with the Debate team.

I shrug.

"Maybe that's why he hasn't asked Evelyn out," David says. "His mom won't let him."

I give David a look like I want to smack him.

"Have you told them about the party yet?" Brent asks.

"No." They take a moment to shake their heads in disapproval. It's like they've rehearsed this movement. "It's just better if they think it's a last-minute surprise thing instead of a planned one." Richard rolls his eyes.

"Your parents, man, like living in prison," David says. "My parents have one rule, 'Call after ten to let us know you're not dead.'"

"It's not Odin's fault his parent like him," Richard says. "Unlike yours." David fumes as Richard flashes him a toothy smile. Brent and I laugh. "I'm kidding."

"Whatever."

"I mean," I say, "they'll be cool with it, right? It's just bowling and food."

Richard shrugs. "What're you asking us for? My parents would be fine with it but we can't even go to your house, so what do we know about your parents?"

"Yeah," David adds, trying to shift the ridicule back to me. "What's up with your house? Do you have severed heads in the freezer or something?"

I give him a blank look. "Yeah," I say, as placidly as possible. "We sneak up from behind and cut their throats." I make a slashing motion with my plastic fork. "You wanna see?"

He grunts. "Whatever, freak."

Brent seizes his chance. "And that's why headshots are always better."

3

"**A**ND THEN MRS. BLANCHET SAT DOWN AGAIN without even knowing that Alvin put gum right on her seat." Andre's laughter breaks up his story. Mom and Dad clearly aren't finding the humor. I do my best not to react either way. "So Alvin said, 'It's so hot today, isn't it?' She said, 'Too hot.' We were all trying so hard not to laugh. Alvin said, 'Hot and sticky.' She just smiled really big and nodded. And my friend Greg looked like he was about to explode."

"That's awful," Mom says, shaking her head.

"No," says Andre, "it was really funny. She's so mean all the time."

"Maybe she's mean because students put gum on her seat."

"No one in class likes her."

"She's just trying to do her job. That doesn't mean she deserves to be tormented."

Andre turns to me. "Isn't that funny, Odin?"

Mom turns as well. Dad merely glances at me as he takes another bite of dinner, as if to say, "You're on your own here, kid."

"I guess it's a little funny," I say, "but not something that anyone should do in their class."

"Doesn't matter if it's funny or not," Mom says.

Dad finishes chewing and looks at each of us one at a time, pulling in our attention.

"It's funny," he says. Mom leers at him. "But there a lot of things that are funny which should never happen."

"I didn't even do it!" Andre protests.

"And we're very happy you didn't," says Mom.

The conversation dies as we all return to dinner, Bulgogi, a recipe that Dad picked up while he was serving in Korea a long time ago. It's marinated beef with garlic and green peppers but calling it "Bulgogi" makes it sound a lot fancier. Kinda like how "Canadian bacon" makes "ham" more exotic and "pâté" sounds much better than "meat paste." Same item, different names, altered idea.

Dad's never been terribly talkative about his experiences in Korea. I observed a bit of it for myself, before I knew better, and it looks like it was a lot of sitting around and preparing for something you hope never happens, but secretly wish would happen, if only so that the time spent preparing wouldn't feel wasted. He often talked to his fellow soldiers about what it would be like if North Korea actually invaded South. Horrific, they'd said, disastrous, bloody, a global calamity the scale of which no one could really estimate— although not in those exact words, it was more like, "A total clusterfuck." Still, after a couple of years of drills and training, a few from his troop longed for a shelling or a short-range rocket launch at a deserted island just to give them something to do. Dad never thought of it that way. He always said that he'd take boring order over exciting chaos anytime.

"Odin," Mom says. She waits for me to swallow before continuing. "Have you given any more though to college?"

"Not really. Concentrating on finals first."

It isn't finals that's keeping me from thinking about college. It's the idea that for some stupid reason this one decision made when I'm through less than a quarter of my life will determine the remaining three quarters. That's a lot of pressure to put on a teenager, especially when it's basically the first independent decision I'll get to make. Of course, independent decision or not, that hasn't stopped my parents from trying to influence me.

"Good," Dad says, "Then we expect straight A's." He looks at me with a snide grin that shows he's only half joking.

"Just remember the deal, dear," Mom says.

"Whatever money's left in your college fund is yours, but only if there's money left." Given the amount of tuition, plus its likelihood to rise, and a worst case scenario of no scholarships, this stipulation leaves only in-state, public universities. Then much more money would be left if I lived at home instead of on campus.

"Do I have a college fund too?" Andre asks.

"Of course."

"So then what if I don't go to college?"

"Your mother and I take an expensive vacation," Dad says just before taking another bite.

"But it's mine."

"It's yours to spend on school. And that's all. What's left is bonus," Mom says. Original intent, not variation.

"I'm gonna find the cheapest school I can," Andre says. "Right, Odin?" I shake my head.

It's a clever trick, but also a bit self-defeating in that Andre probably would choose the cheapest school. Or he would at this point. He's only thirteen. He hasn't even started high school yet. He has no idea how much change he's in for. Friends, classes, interests, likes and dislikes. Everything is fluid. And that's why making a life-altering decision right after high school is so damn intimidating.

The funny thing about my family is that even though I was adopted, I look a bit like Mom and Dad. Mostly in the generic ways: dark skin and hair, similar body type, although much smaller than Dad, the big elements that group people together. However, their eyes are almost black while mine are hazel, even yellow at times. Andre and I look like we could be brothers, even with the eyes. He's a kid and hasn't yet developed individual features, in the way that pictures of old people as children look nothing like what they later become. Their faces are smaller and rounder as kids, without the angles, lines and creases that come with age. Makes me wonder what I'll look like in my thirties or forties.

Andre can look at Dad for some idea, the way

his jaw widens outwardly from under his ears or the cheekbones pressed back almost to the very ends of his face. Or Mom, the sharp curve from her brow to her nose, and the similar one from bottom lip to chin. He can have some idea of what his finished face will be. I can't. I barely remember my parents beyond a pair of voices, one low and raspy and the other high and melodic. I tried looking back on them once but it was . . . too much. Every memory leads to that last day. Can't change the past.

"It'll be here sooner than you think," says Mom. "Odin?"

"What?"

"College. It'll be here sooner than you think. Just a year away."

"I know."

"All right," she says, in that way that means anything other than "all right."

"College will come," Dad says, "but there's a more immediate concern." He leans his folded arms onto the table. He squints directly at me. "Something of far greater importance and urgency than school."

I cock my head at him.

"What do you want to do for your birthday?" Andre laughs.

"Oh, yeah!" says Mom.

Dad continues, easing out of his masqueraded intensity. "I was thinking about maybe a movie and then dinner at Marzano. Or," to Mom, "what's that place we went to that one time? The Cajun place?"

"On the Bayou," she offers.

"Right. It was good." To me, "You ever had Cajun food?"

"What's Cajun?" Andre asks.

"It's the kind of food down in N'Orleans, where Grandma and Grandpa are from. It's French-Southern."

"That might be a little too spicy for the kids," Mom says.

"Oh, I think they can handle a little spice. As Paw Paw would say, 'Put a li'l bit o' hair on them boys' chests,'" he says in a mimic of Grandpa Lewis's accent.

"Ewwww," says Andre.

"So a movie, dinner, and dessert after. Maybe try out that new—"

"Actually," I say at last, almost sad to put end their plans, "Brent and Richard and them kinda already planned something. They just told me about it today."

"Oh," says Mom. "Good." She pauses before continuing. "What do they want to do?"

"Bowling and food. Nothing too big."

"That sounds fun. Do you know who's going?" she asks.

"Probably just like the bowling team and the usual guys." I purposefully use the term "guys."

"Maybe if you're not home too late we can all do something together after," she says.

"Nah," says Dad, "let him stay out with his friends." He pretends to sniffle. "We'll be fine."

"Can I come?" Andre asks.

"Uhhhh . . . " I hedge.

"Let Odin have that day," Dad says. "We'll find something more fun to do without him."

"Yeah," says Mom, "good. Have fun."

She's hurt, even if she has no reason or right to feel that way. I've spent every other birthday with them, even those which included my friends. It was always at a park or something with their supervision. Even last year when Evelyn brought me cupcakes she'd made, they were right there. Hovering around.

"Just do me one favor," Dad says.

"What's that?"

"Wipe the alley with your friends."

I smile. "You got it."

"And speaking of wiping, if you're done you boys can start clearing the table."

Andre sighs as he slides his chair out. He takes

his plate and glass around the counter where the brown tile of the dining room meets the white tile of the kitchen.

"Bet you didn't see that coming," says Dad.

"It was very clever," I reply, removing my silverware and dishes as well.

"You hear that, hon?" Dad says, I assume to Mom across the table. "He called me clever."

"You must be very proud," she says flatly.

"Best compliment I've had since the coffee lady at work called me a 'bold espresso,'" he deadpans.

I chuckle as I place my plate in the sink.

"What's funny?" Andre asks.

"Nothing," I say. "Don't forget your utensils."

4

MATTER AND ENERGY. MATTER AND ENERGY. THAT'S what stands out from tonight's physics reading. Chapter 11: Matter and Energy. Matter and energy. What's the matter? Not worth the energy.

Not that the subject is boring, far from it, but the text certainly does its best to make the subject seem boring. The text uses the basest definition of the term to create broad assumptions. Matter: physical material made up of atoms and which possesses mass. Does that mean there is no matter in things which have no mass? What about atoms themselves, are they not matter? If not, then is anything made from atoms therefore not matter? These are the kinds of questions that the textbook tends to skip. And the kinds of questions that a teacher will label you a "smart ass" for asking. Doesn't a greater understanding of matter matter?

Of course, for me the process of studying is less about absorbing the information in the book than in having it present at some point in time. When I get stuck on a test or on the homework, I can simply look back into my memory or someone else's, if I can hold a solid enough picture of them in my mind, and locate the information. I trace back to a time when the information was there and then pause the image, like a freeze frame. However, this is for the past and only up to a few moments before the present. I guess that's where the present becomes the past, or something like that. Either way, never the future. I guess because the future is still being determined by actions in the present, or whatever. I can't exactly explain it, not like there's anyone who can spell it all out for me, not even anyone who really knows about this other than Dr. Burnett, and

I haven't seen her in years. It's quite nice actually, having Wikipedia wired into my brain, except my edition is accurate and doesn't have people fighting over the latest edits. So, while waiting for the information to come of use, I flip through pages of boring text, skimming over the words as quickly as possible so that I can concentrate on more important things.

I hold my hand flat and watch the pencil rotate. A lot of my classmates like to spin their pencils when they're bored. I never got the hang of the full spin, the one that turns through a finger snap with the pencil landing neatly between the two fingers after one rotation, but none of my classmates can do the kind of spin that I can; the pencil is four inches above my palm. I move my fingers as though pushing the pencil through the air. I don't know if my motion has any effect but it helps in visualizing the pencil's movement. I never touch it. The pencil appears to have no mass, therefore it doesn't matter.

It's only been a few months since I first noticed I could do this. Up and down movement is easy, as is side to side. Rotation has taken some practice. I've gotten to the point where I can do it while slightly distracted, such as while skimming boring physics reading with its reductive definitions. Flipping the pencil end over end requires more concentration. I figure this is because it's not a motion a pencil tends to have, not even when spun by bored students. I save the more complicated movements for after I'm done skimming the chapter. It's my reward for cataloguing another several pages of potential exam material for use later.

I tried with the books once. Again, up and down was easy, side to side as well, but not much else. I could barely get the cover open while the book was in the air without it dropping onto my desk with a thud loud enough that Mom knocked on door to ask what happened. I said the chapter was about gravity and required a demonstration by dropping it. She's smart enough to know it was bullshit, I mean, the text would never include anything as interesting as that, but my explanation got her to leave without any suspicion. That I know of.

My trouble with the book is why I haven't risked anything heavier yet. Not my desk with the computer on top, the bookshelf, the bed, or the dresser. Hopefully I can work my way up to those in a few months. Maybe even get to the point where the next time Kevin gets in my face, I really can toss him to half court. That would be a lot more badass than a headshot.

I lean my chair back to look at the bottom of the book. The thin lines of each page run along its length appearing inseparable. Of course they aren't. I stare closely at the top page and imagine the feeling of lifting that single sheet between my fingers. As close as the pages may seem, there is still space between them. A tiny infinity between two distinct ends. I place my hand at the side of the book and imagine the page lifting. It doesn't move.

I try again by waving my hand over the top as though flipping the pages. The bent bottom corner flaps slightly. Might've been the breeze from my hand.

I close my eyes and breathe out slowly, probably making that bent corner flutter once again. It's such an easy motion, one that I've seen and caused millions of times: page lifts from the outside edge, up and over, with the inside following. The bent corner begins to elevate. It continues up, pulling the entire side with it. I arc my hand over it mimicking the motion I'd like for the page to make. It does. On the next page is a picture of a baseball pitcher mid-release, the moment before the ball flies through the air.

Great, I have accomplished in two minutes of intense concentration what takes two seconds of physical contact. So hopefully I won't have to fend bullies off again within the next, say, fifty fucking years!

The word "good" pops into my mind as though floating under my vision.

I skim down the next two pages. Conversion of

kinetic to potential energy. Basically the stuff Zeller covered in class today, stated again for those who didn't listen during class. As though those who didn't listen during class would bother doing the reading.

The words *making* followed by *progress* enter my head like whispers.

I look around. The little television on the dresser is turned off. The door is closed but not locked; my parents don't like for it to be locked. Unmade bed still unmade. Spiderman poster on the wall—the comic book Spiderman, not the movie one—still there even though I haven't read the comics since starting high school. Seemed too childish. The issues from when I used to collect remain on the bottom row of the bookshelf while the other shelves overflow with thick novels and reference books Mom and Dad have given me for birthdays and Christmases, along with the two *Playboy*s Richard smuggled to me last year, which have each been opened more often than all of those thick novels and references combined. I slowly pull up the window blinds to see if anyone is out there. Just the night, the knotty wooden fence between our house and the Aukermans', and my reflection staring back.

I return to the book open in front of me and finish skimming. I flip the page over without any trouble. "Good" enters my mind again, bouncing around my thoughts as though trying to find something to attach itself to. I flip the next page without skimming. The next one as well. As easy as flicking a finger. I flip back two pages to where my skimming left off.

Odin.

I look around again. Still nothing. I stand up to check right outside the door. Empty hallway and nothing else. Even so, even with nothing, I feel my heart pound a little heavier.

I pull the window blinds up again and still see nothing but my reflection staring back. I wake up the computer to make sure some incredibly personal pop-up ads haven't appeared. I open the closet. There's the old toy chest that was here the day I arrived, on the floor underneath my coats, jackets, and the suit I had to wear to Paw Paw's funeral hanging from the rack. I place my hand on the back of the television to make sure it's completely cool. I toss the sheet and the pillows from the bed, though it couldn't be more of a mess. Then I sit down again, still looking at the surroundings as though they will change right before my eyes. I know there's nothing here, but I feel like there is.

Has it been so long that you do not remember me?

"What the hell?" I say out loud. My eyes dart around the room.

Do not worry.

"What's happening?" I say to the nothing that I see. I feel my shoulder and neck tense. I blink quickly.

It is just me. There's still nothing. The words enter directly into my mind. I place both hands on the sides of my head—over my ears—like they'll keep the words from entering. The voice sounds exactly like mine, if thoughts can have sound.

Wendell.

"Wendell?" I say. A slight shake rolls from my head to my feet.

There was only once when I thought he was real. My first day in this house, just over a month after the accident. I always imagined him as being like me, like a twin, but knew he was nothing other than an imaginary friend. Something I'd grown out of years ago. Like Spiderman.

I knew you remembered.

Okay, no need to worry, Dr. Burnett said Wendell is the sign of a healthy but overactive imagination. He was made up when I was alone and confused over what happened with my parents and needed someone to relate to. Nothing more. No matter.

I resume skimming the next two pages, totally normal, barely focusing on more than the general shape of the words. The tall letters and those with tails stand as outliers among the others. The variants.

The deviants. They're what give the words their shape. They're what make the words recognizable. But shape doesn't provide definition, and I can't get myself to focus on the specific letters.

Still not interested in talking to your oldest friend?

He can't read my thoughts, can't feel the thump in my chest, but he can tell I'm agitated.

Or afraid that my being here will make people insult you again?

The pencil slowly rises from the table again, without my trying. I cover it with my hand. I close my eyes tightly.

Have you told any of them about me since then?

Coping mechanism. Probably anxiety over college. Overactive imagination. Focus and he'll go away. Just like he did before.

I could look for myself.

I breathe in deep. "No," I whisper, hoping no one in the house will hear me talking to myself. They never seemed to before. "Not since Kevin."

Kevin. You two were friends.

"Yeah," I say back, even though I know I shouldn't.

Kevin looked so lost that first day in third grade. He sat in class with his shoulders hunched and head down as though if he tried hard enough, he'd able to fold into himself and disappear. Then, during the second week of school, he showed up with a big bandage at his left temple, covering part of his hairline. The other kids found it impossible not to hound him about it. They stared at it as he walked into class, sat at the benches outside, and every time the teacher turned her back on us. He was like a wounded gazelle thrown to the cheetahs. Each of them was ready to pounce.

Maybe it was because I was one of the only kids smaller than he was—this was before he sprouted like a weed in eighth grade—but he didn't cower away when I approached the curb where he sat alone after school every day while waiting for his dad to pick him up. I pointed at the fresh bandage at the very edge of his face.

"You fell," I said.

He stared at me. He didn't move but he looked ready to at any moment.

"Running in your house. You slipped and hit the bottom stair. You got nine stitches."

His eyes grew. "How do you know that?"

"I have a friend who tells me things sometimes."

"Who?"

"A friend. You can't see him. Only I can see him. But it's okay. He told me to talk to you because you're nice and scared and you shouldn't be scared."

"I'm tired of everyone asking about it."

"It's a mystery," I said, reciting words Wendell whispered to me. "Once they know what it is, they won't be interested anymore."

"But it's stupid." He sulked down behind his

oversized Winnie the Pooh backpack. "They'll make fun of me more."

"Tell them it's something else. You got into a fight with this other kid and totally beat him up."

He sat motionless for a moment until his eyes flicked up at me. "Which kid?"

I shrugged. "Make something up."

"Ummmm . . . like what?"

I dropped my own ridiculously large bag to the ground with the force of almost one hundred and two joules. I sat next to him on the grass along the curb. Winnie the Pooh stared out at the road.

"We'll tell people that there's this kid in your neighborhood who's always causing trouble for the other kids. One day you yelled at him to stop being mean. You started fighting and he hit you once and that's why you got cut, but you hit him back and broke his nose and his jaw and cut his eye open really bad. And now he doesn't bother anyone anymore."

" . . . You think they will believe me?"

"They will if we both say it. I can say I was there when it happened."

"But I don't know you."

"I'm Odin Lewis," I said. "Who're you?"

"Kevin Clark."

"Clarke like the city?"

"Kind of, but spelled different. My great-grandpa owned a bunch of stuff around here for a long time and then sold it to the government to build the base out by the lake."

"Now we know each other."

Kevin sat up and smiled.

Everyone wanted to know more about the fight but I told Kevin not to add anything else. It would be more believable that way. The story grew on its own. The other kid spent two days in the hospital, had to have rhinoplasty, got a glass eye, was taken out of school to heal before transferring to a new one. Our classmates took the story to completely new places. The only ones who knew the truth were Kevin and me.

That's how it really happened. I don't have to remember it. I can see it.

That is funny.

I stared at the open book in front of me on the desk in my room. I wait for Wendell to continue, for his words to again enter my mind as though a ghost were whispering in my ear. When no follow-up comes, I foolishly prompt one.

"Funny?"

I remember when I was your only friend. Then Kevin came along. You did not want to talk to me anymore. He replaced me. Now Kevin has new friends and does not talk to you. He replaced you.

"You told me to talk to him," I mutter like a curse.

It is not "haha" funny, but there is an amusing parallel to it all.

I don't remember him speaking this way. So rigid

and formal. His vocabulary has increased over time as well. Probably because mine has. It makes sense that the voice in my head would progress in the same way I have. Surprising, though, that he speaks so differently from me. Not that it matters.

"Could you please stop bothering me? I'm trying to concentrate." I speak politely, calmly, in control. Bad things happen when I lose control.

He's quiet as I skim down to the bottom of the page. I turn to the next by pinching the corner of the paper.

Do it the real way.

"Do what?" I snap.

Turn the page the real way. The way you are supposed to.

"I did."

No. The way you *are supposed to. The way only you can.*

"I'm trying to study here." I shouldn't engage. I know I shouldn't.

He laughs. An electric surge rushes from the

center of my head to the tips of my fingers. Not painful. Not pleasant. Noticeable.

There are more important things to study.

I don't reply. I close my eyes again. Focus. He'll go away.

Like the real way to turn a page. You cannot become advanced if you do not learn the basics.

"Advanced what?" I immediately curse myself for replying.

You will get there.

I sigh. I look up to catch my reflection through the blinds in the window. Must look silly talking to an imaginary childhood friend again. No, talking to myself. Sixteen, almost seventeen years old, and unable to grow up.

There is something you want to ask me. I keep the pencil in hand as I return to the physics book. Still have twenty pages of AP Euro to skim after this.

Why not just ask?

Energy—I focus on the word in the book— can't be created or destroyed. It can be converted and transferred, such as when two masses collide, changing potential energy into kinetic energy. Mass, matter, energy. Wendell does not have mass, he does not matter, he is a waste of energy. Stop focusing on him.

If I am the result of trauma, as that doctor claimed—He says doctor in a peculiar way, as though there should be quotation marks around it—*then you should know that I will never go away. I may disappear for a while, but I will always be back.*

Moving on, Dr. Burnett said, was the hardest part. Recognizing the fact that the life we had known before was gone and could never come back. It could take years to fully recover because we don't know the extent of our trauma. For us, trauma is normal.

Wendell was my way of dealing with the loss of my parents. He was the guilt and anger I didn't know I was feeling at the time. He was why I knocked Colin Griffin down the stairs in third grade, breaking the boy's arm in two places. It wasn't my choice, it was this character I'd imagined in my mind that urged me to act out. Burnett said I'd be better once I didn't need him anymore. I was, too. After he disappeared, it was much easier to open up to others. Or at least as much as I open up to them now.

I am not a construct. You know that. I have a different purpose.

Deep breaths. Control.

And so do you.

"Fine," I spit out louder than I probably should. "Where did you go? Why are you back? Did you meet Elvis and/or Tupac while you were there?" I'm actually kind of interested to know, if only to admire the extent of my own imagination.

I was somewhere else.

Well, that was disappointing.

Somewhere no one else has ever been. You did not need me then so I let you be.

"Boohoo," I say, a viciousness creeping into my tone. "I must have a truly unique sense of self-pity if my imaginary friend is trying to send me on a guilt trip."

Odin, when did you become mean? We were friends. I was there when you needed me. I was there to talk to when no one else was. I understood what you were going through when your parents died. How it caused you to act. I was here for you from the first day in this new town. All alone. Living with strangers.

I sigh. As messed up as it is, it's true. He was the only, let's say "person," that I could be honest with for a long time. While I had to smile and be polite to Mom and Dad, and especially with Andre, I could be angry with Wendell. He encouraged me to get it out and never judged me for it. It wasn't the best thing to do, but I needed it. I needed the catharsis. Otherwise, I might not be the well-adjusted teen that I am, staring at myself in the bedroom window while having a quiet chat with the voice in my head. Yup, perfectly normal.

I left because you had adjusted to your new life

and did not need me anymore. So I went somewhere else. But not far, in case you needed me again.

"So, you moved from, like, my frontal lobe to my . . . whatever part of the brain stores long term memory?" I run through last year's biology class like rewinding a DVR. I pause on the diagram of the brain. "Cortex," I say calmly after a couple of seconds. Sarcasm. It's safer than anger, and usually just as satisfying.

You could say that.

"And you're back now because . . . ?"

You need me.

"For . . . ?"

For what comes next. You will have a new life soon. One that nobody else can help you with.

"College?" I say. "Thanks but I don't think my imaginary friend will help me adjust. In fact, talking to myself could be a good reason no else would talk to me."

I feel his chuckle in my entire body.

You were never so defensive before. Why the closed mind?

"Trying to make sure I don't lose it."

There is something much more important approaching. When it comes, you will know. And you will need me.

"Why would I need you now if I didn't before?"

Because no one else understands you like I do.

I laugh. "You sound like a character from every after-school special ever. 'Oh, I'm such a rebel, no one understands just how much of a rebel I am. I'm gonna write bad poetry, play guitar, get gauges in my ears, and all that other cliché shit so everyone will see that I'm such a rebel. Much, much rebel.'" I don't know why I say that, but I do.

He doesn't reply.

I clench my jaw a couple of times and watch in the window how the shadows appear at the ends of my cheeks. There was a time when I thought my face looked best this way. I walked around all day with my teeth pressed tightly together. After two days it hurt to chew.

Are you done mocking me?

"If I say yes, does that mean I can't change my mind later?"

You have no idea just how much you will need me.

"Well, while you're in my head, why not just show me? Save us both the time."

We do not work that way. You know this.

He told me this years ago. Even though he exists in my brain, a brain which until tonight I thought was functioning quite well, he doesn't have access to my thoughts. Nor do I have access to his. He said there might be a way to change this, but he advised against it at the time. I'd oppose it now. He can see the past, just like I can, but not the future, just like I can't. We're essentially two people sharing the same living space. In proximity, but entirely separate. Maybe that's why he doesn't talk like me.

There are things you need to know. That is why

I have returned. I can teach you what no one else can.

"Can you get to the point so I can finish my work? These books aren't going to skim themselves."

Benjamin and Aida, your parents, are not who they say they are.

I wait for more. Again, no more comes. "Is that it?"

Nothing.

"Well, yeah," I say with all the awe of hearing someone confess that the sky is, in fact, blue. "I mean technically that's true, they say they're my parents, and they are by legal and emotional means, but they're not in the biological or genetic se—"

They are your jailors.

This stops me for a second.

Then I continue. "They can be a bit strict, but I wouldn't call them jailors. Yeah, no Facebook, no friends over, come home directly from school and all that, but it's not like they're feeding me gruel and making me sew shoes with my teeth all day."

You do not know who your real parents are.
You do not know what happened to them.

I see my reflection in the window again. The shadows at the ends of my cheeks. There were reflections and shadows the day of the accident too. The blood on the front grill of the truck. The bodies in the street.

"Wherever you were," I say quietly, between my teeth, "you should go back."

If you are so sure that I am wrong . . .

"I don't fucking need you here," I say, my voice rising.

I feel my nostrils flare. Some kind of feral animal stares back at me in the window, menacing, angry, ready to rip and tear into flesh with its claws. I take a deep breath to calm myself. Then I remember that Mom, Dad, and Andre are all still awake and hope they didn't hear me. I look down to see the book has turned a dozen pages without me noticing.

. . . You can see for yourself.

"No," I say reducing my voice to growling whisper.

You can look at that day.

"I can't." My head shakes back and forth, as though trying to toss him out.

Memory is weak. Memories can change. They, the doctor, your parents—He's speaking with quotation marks again—*have made you afraid of the truth. Conditioned you to never seek it out. But you can see them for what they truly are. You can know.*

"Leave me alone."

You are scared because you know that maybe I am right.

"I'm not scared, I'm just done listening. You're nothing. You're a remnant of a time when I was a frightened child, acting out because there was no other way for me to feel consequential." That's what Burnett told me then. I speak slowly, through gritted teeth. "I will not go back to that."

Prove me wrong and I will never bother you again.

"There's nothing to prove." I'm shaking, like it's cold. Everything is cold. "I will not be that boy again. I am not helpless."

No. You definitely are not . . .

"There is too much in the future to be stuck in the past."

. . . I will make sure of that.

I don't know how, but I know he disappears. Whether it's to this "somewhere else" or to another part of this room we share, I know he's not speaking or listening to me anymore. And I'm glad. Maybe he'll stay away. Like he did before.

In the window a wounded animal stares back. Timid, fearful, ripped at and ready to die. Tearing, in the way no other animal can.

He's just a voice, Dr. Burnett said, an imaginary voice. He can't do anything.

He can't do anything.

5

I USUALLY HAVE TROUBLE SLEEPING. THERE'S TOO MUCH to think about. Then, after thinking about too much when I should be sleeping, I end up tossing around for another hour and worrying about how the next day will be after a night thinking instead of sleeping. I wonder if I'll end up sleeping in class and which class it'll be. Mrs. Wilson keeps smelling salts in her desk to wake sleeping students with. Mr. Murakami used his dry erase markers until one student jerked up too quickly and received a red ink streak on his upper lip that looked like a nosebleed. Usually it's around the time that my mind drifts off to aliens or talking furniture that I later realize I've finally fallen asleep. I like being reminded that sleep is possible.

Instead of aliens or worries about falling asleep in class, my mind wanders in a different direction. Wendell. Not exactly what he said, but tangential to it. The idea that I could know whatever I want. I could learn whatever there is to know about Mom or Dad or Evelyn or anyone else, but observing them would be too much. It would be a violation of trust. I should focus on someone with whom there has already been a violation. Where there is no trust.

It was two months ago when Kevin and David were talking, for some reason, as they exited the school. As David was about to veer off to the bus stop, Kevin asked where David lived. David told him his address: 115th, right before Alva. It was on Kevin's way home, he said.

"A different route than I usually take but not a problem. Unless you *want* to ride the bus like a dumbass," Kevin said.

"Fuck no," David replied. "There's this old guy

who wears a black suit and tie who always sits in the back row and yells 'hello' and 'goodbye' to everyone," he said as they cut through the grass in front of the school toward the street, which curved around campus. "He's fucking weird."

Kevin's car is a silver Toyota Sequoia. Biggest car that any of the students at the school have, he bragged after opening the doors with the little remote attached to a bottle opener keychain. "Backseat big and low enough for two people to be on without anyone knowing," he said after they'd buckled in. "Until she starts to cum."

David laughed too much at this. The kind of laugh people make when they want someone to *think* they know exactly what the other person is talking about.

That's when the conversation directed toward me and Evelyn.

"You know anything about that?" Kevin asked. "Something going on?"

"Nah, he's like obsessed with her but she

probably doesn't give a shit about him. I only really hang out with him because Brent and Richard do. He's pretty lame."

"We were friends in grade school, but he became such a nerd," said he of the giant, square glasses with fake lenses. Kevin leaned back with one elbow on the driver's side window and barely held onto the bottom of the wheel. "Like, he wouldn't leave me alone. Every weekend he wanted to hang out. Like I was his only friend. Like, he even made up a friend when he was a kid."

David gawks.

"For real, yo. He had an imaginary friend. He was such a freaky little kid that he actually had to imagine another person just to have someone to talk to. He would like throw shit around too. We'd come into a room after him and there'd be like papers on the ground and shit and he'd be muttering something to himself. Then he'd be like, 'I didn't do it.'"

David laughs. "For real?"

"Yeah, I mean, we were like friends and shit, but

I just felt sorry for the kid. I thought that maybe if we were friends, then he wouldn't come after me when he finally snapped, you know what I mean?"

David laughed too much again. "Me too. I mean, like I feel sorry for him too. That's the only reason I, like, talk to him and stuff."

"Thought you said it was because of Brent and Richard."

"Yeah, but, I mean like, we all feel sorry for him. He just kinda wandered into our group one day and wouldn't leave. Now we feel too bad to tell him to go away."

Kevin laughs then. "Same thing happened to me, man, same exact thing. I just got so sick of it, you know? I sacrificed all of grade school and middle school to that kid. Wasn't about to do that with high school." He rolled his head around as he said, "Hell no."

"Yeah," said David, "probably next year we'll find a way to get away from him. Move to a new place to eat lunch or something. I haven't even seen him outside of the cafeteria since like second semester of sophomore year. I don't take fucking AP classes."

Kevin asked which way to turn on 115th. David directed him from there.

Like Dad always said, there's a reason people keep certain things private. And that's why I can't get myself to observe my parents, or Evelyn. I don't want them to change.

I roll over to check the clock on my phone. It says 4:30 a.m. Two more hours before the phone's alarm goes off and it's time to get ready for yet another day of school. Doubt I'll get any sleep tonight. Too much to think about. Too much to not think about.

At least I've made it past lunch without once nodding off in class. There was a scare during calculus when Mrs. Henderson was once again lecturing on calculating differentials in curved lines. It's pretty boring, but Mom wanted me to take the subject before senior year so my final grade will be on my record before applying to universities. I never pay much attention in that class since the answers are there whenever I need them.

My mind wandered to how so many of the various functions of a graph start at a common origin but then curve into different directions with the slightest tweak of an infinitesimal, a number so small it's little more than nothing. Lines swing wildly by altering even the smallest number. It's basically chaos theory, calculating an infinite number of possibilities following only one undetectably small change. See, that to me is interesting. It's a shame Mrs. Henderson never puts the subject in those terms. Instead she just talks about raw numbers without even attempting to tie them into any practical application. It wasn't until I started taking physics that I saw how algebra applies to the real world. Maybe students would be more interested in the subject if they felt like they were getting something out of it other than looking good on university applications. Instead, we fight off the urge to sleep. And try not to think about the things that we can't help thinking about.

Wendell said there were much more important things. More important than college, especially, but more important than a lot of things I imagine.

Then I mused on how funny it is that infinitesimal, an amount so small that it can't be detected, begins with the word infinite, a number so large it can't be calculated. That made me chuckle. And that's when Mrs. Henderson asked if there was something I'd like to share with the class. There was no danger of falling asleep anymore.

Mr. Zeller is talking about velocity in a vacuum versus velocity in wind resistance and how to calculate for both. Numbers thirteen and thirty-four on the exam. He turns his back to write on the board.

I look around. Brandon in the back has his book propped up in front of him as though everyone doesn't know that he's been sleeping for the last ten minutes. William has his hand over the drawing in his notebook of what was originally supposed to be an eagle but has since become some sort of winged monster with a giant penis. Miles is also drawing but on a sheet of printer paper. He erases a line from the hand of a female superhero in skin-tight clothes. Her hip juts out in one direction and her leg in another. He cocks his head to see if it looks right. It doesn't. He's been using every other class to substitute for the AP art course that was cancelled last year. Erin is writing a note that she'll pass to Denise after class is over to read in the next one. The five students in the front, Anne and them, the overachievers or suck-ups, depending on how nice you want to be, are scribbling notes furiously. She got an A- in bio last year and has to make up for that or her parents won't love her anymore. Something like that.

Victor Scheffer said, "Although nature needs thousands or millions of years to create a new species, man needs only a few dozen years to destroy one." It's right there on the wall, under his picture. I've read it probably a few dozen times, to use his words.

Then there's Evelyn, head angled down, eyes angled up, reading along as Zeller talks. She keeps her pen ready at any moment. She once told me that her goal this year was just to maintain a good GPA going into applications. Didn't mean she *had* to get straight As, although that would be nice, but less than a B isn't acceptable. I replied that it's hard to get less than a B at this school. She laughed and said, "It is for you."

There's Wendell in my mind again. Much more important things. Funny thing is, I don't need to watch any of my classmates as they fidget and sleep and draw their way through the hour we spend sitting in this room. I can see it in front of me. Everything I *need* to know is right here. It's not in private conversations behind my back.

Kevin and David's conversation plays again in my head. David is supposed to be my friend. At least he is in person. Kevin is an enemy. Is "enemy" the right word? Makes it sound like we're working every day to destroy each other. I know we've fought, but I can't imagine having an *enemy*. If there was a real threat—if we were both on the street and some guy walked up with a gun—I don't think he'd push me in front of him or anything. That's rather enemy-like.

It makes sense that there would be other guys interested in Evelyn. She has mixture of sweet and mischievous that she rarely shows but is always welcome, similar to how lights dance off her dark eyes. The button nose, runner's legs, eyebrows that arch steadily until just before the outer end and then slope sharply downward. She's like one of Miles's superhero girls, only without the deformed hips and giant tits. The interest makes sense, but that doesn't mean I have to like it.

I can imagine what it would be like if Kevin or someone like him could do what I can. Look into the past, float, and turn objects. He'd be showing off constantly. He'd probably walk through the halls with his pencil spinning on his fingertip like a basketball. He'd shout out everybody's most embarrassing secrets to the whole school. He'd probably spend all day and night watching the girls showering and getting dressed. Hell, he wouldn't even show up to school. He'd stay home finding new ways to humiliate people. Again, I could find out everything. He's lucky I don't. He's lucky I'm better than he is.

I wonder, if given the choice between Kevin and me, which would she choose? He's taller, I'll give him that, but his ears stick out and his face looks like a big rectangle, so I'm better looking. At least I like to think so. She did call me cute at least once. It was a month ago, during her nightly phone call with Maria. She said that she saw me on the street that afternoon while she was riding with her mom. They stopped so I could cross in front of them. She liked the way I waved quickly before stepping into the road. I didn't see her in the car, it's just what I always do. She didn't tell me this. I felt bad immediately after for seeing it and for again breaking a promise I made to myself long ago that I wouldn't learn anything about her that she didn't want to share with me herself. Still, remembering the way her voice raised for "so cute" made me smile for a week.

If she's called me cute once then she's probably called me that again. She was quiet yesterday but she's usually that way when Maria's around. What did Maria tell her after she caught me staring?

They turned around to walk to the lunchroom. Maria asked her how class was. Evelyn said it was okay. Nothing exciting. They talked a bit more, got lunch, sat down with the others, they talked about classes and shoes, blah, blah, blah. She watched as I walked over to my table with Brent and sat down. Maria laughed.

"What?" Evelyn asked.

Maria smiled and gestured with her head in my direction. Evelyn shook her head and poked at her food.

"He was staring at you the whole time in the hallway too, you know."

"I know."

Maria smiled again, wiggled a little in her seat.

"Nothing's happened," Evelyn said quietly.

"But he did invite you to his birthday party."

"He probably invited a lot of people."

"I doubt that."

"Still, doesn't mean anything." Evelyn looked around to see if any of the other girls were listening. They were taking about Mrs. Bourne's new hair color. "You're coming too."

"Yeah, but since I'm just coming for you does that mean I have to, like, get him a present or something?"

"I don't think so."

"Are you getting him something?" She stretched out the word "you" for added emphasis.

"Yeah. I don't know what yet."

"Get him condoms."

Evelyn's mouth dropped open.

"Oh come on. You know that's all they think about."

Evelyn looked at the others again.

"It's not like that. Not only like that."

I've gone too far.

No more snooping into her life or anyone else important to me. Besides, if she ever finds out I'd been watching her personal conversations—other than the obvious questions of "How?" and "No, seriously, how?"—she'd probably feel so betrayed that any feelings she may have would be gone. No one is that forgiving.

It was her hairpin that first caught my eye during the freshman orientation we had to attend before beginning at this school. A big, cartoonish skull with the three pointy teeth sticking out and a lightning-bolt crack down the top of the head. She told me later it was from an anime she liked a couple years before.

I also remember the white, sleeveless shirt with the black collar and the top two buttons undone.

The third button had a frayed string sticking out from behind. She had small silver earrings and blue, low-top sneakers double knotted. One of the aglets was cracked along its length. I remember the little pimple she had on the left side of her forehead. She was a couple of inches shorter then, less developed, and her cheeks were rounder. That's probably where the squirrel cheeks image came from. First impressions and all. The skull hairpin didn't stand out so much as the sensibility hinted at by wearing it. It was incongruous with the sweet looking girl with the round cheeks and big eyes. Even the skull was a bit askew, round and cute, not an angular symbol of death. It seemed to say, "I'll kill you, nicely."

Evelyn sat two desks away from me when we broke into smaller groups. We didn't talk at all. We didn't even face each other. This before she knew anyone at the school. I only knew Kevin.

I'm among the last to leave the class, at least the last of the non-suck-up students who semi-circle around to ask questions and discuss ways to raise their grade from a solid A to a rock solid A. Waiting is a habit I picked up pretty quickly in freshman year as a way of avoiding the crowd at the door. It's not like we're going anywhere soon. Not until our four years are up. Why rush?

I spot Evelyn and Maria in the hall as they turn toward their final class of the day. Then I'm blindsided by another student. The hit spins me halfway around. I reach for a locker to keep me up.

"Watch out, Oddin."

I sigh.

There's a lingering impact in my left shoulder from the hit. My back aches from where this heavy bag wrenched around. He could have been standing there, waiting for me to step out so he could pop me. I push myself up. I turn to look at him, big ears, long face, square glasses, dumbass spiky hair and all.

"Shithead," he says.

I can't help remembering the last time we were this close to each other. That day on the basketball court. I look back into the room where Zeller remains surrounded by the overachievers.

I gesture with one hand for Kevin to pass by.

"Move!" he replies.

I make the same gesture again. This time with both hands. Other students turn to watch as they continue on their paths without running into each other.

"Get out of my way," Kevin says quietly, trying to sound menacing but making it harder to understand the words.

"I'm letting you go around," I say.

"You go around."

"You're the one in such a hurry," I say. "Continue."

I don't look at him. I don't need to. I can feel his stare like a lamp a foot away from my face. Other students walk by slowly, the way rubberneckers pass the scene of an accident.

You could do something about this right now.

"Shut up," I say out loud. Kevin shoves me down. This time the movement is too fast, the bag too heavy and off balance. I hit the floor with my right hand first. My right knee hits next. There's a dull pain in the knee joint, like getting hit by a baseball.

"Don't tell me to shut up, Oddin."

I get a picture in my mind of standing up slowly, uncurling like a snake from a basket. Bringing my head up last to stare Kevin directly in the eyes. Shoving him back so hard he flies ten feet and slides half as many across the floor.

You could. If you want.

Instead I push myself up to my feet. I involuntarily rub at my sore knee. I feel the heft of my backpack, all one hundred fifty joules of it, pulling toward the floor. The other students have stopped rubbernecking and started spectating. I wish I could disappear completely. Poof into thin air and take the memories of this moment with me. But things are never clean. No one is that forgetful.

"Hey," Zeller's voice comes from the room next to us. "What's going on out there?"

"Nothing," Kevin says as he steps around me. Finally. The other students move noticeably faster. The overachievers file out the door one by one and walk on without stopping. I move on as well.

I catch Evelyn before she disappears around the corner. She shakes her head pitifully.

In front of everyone. Tossed to the ground like a little kid. Did nothing. Teacher had to yell for it stop it. This fucking sucks. Right in front of everyone. They'll all be laughing at me tomorrow.

They should laugh.

"Not you," I say out loud. I'm trying to decompress on my bed back home after a long, humiliating day at school before making it look like I have to do homework. Instead of being alone with my thoughts, I get Wendell yakking at me. After years of silence, most of my life so far, he comes back and won't shut up. "I'd like to be alone right now."

You could do something to stop all of them from laughing. But you refuse to.

I sigh. "I thought you were here to help."

I am.

"Well, you're not, so either stop trying or get a new dictionary because you clearly don't understand the word 'help.'"

You have no idea what you can do.

I close my eyes. I see myself knocked to the ground. Lying painfully on my side. One leg extended. One leg bent underneath. A pathetic little child as the others watch. They laugh to themselves quietly. He's so weak, they think, probably won't do anything about it. Such a pussy. There's Evelyn in the back. She shakes her head in dismissal. Even she stayed to watch.

You have power.

I look up at my bedroom ceiling again. A weird brown spot has been there for years. Looks like dirt. It shouldn't be possible for dirt to cling to a ceiling, and yet there it is. Down the wall and there's Spiderman, swinging at me from between two buildings.

You can make them all stop.

I don't know why I still have that poster on the wall. I tried to take it down once, about a year after I stopped reading the comics, but I felt guilty. As though he, Spiderman, would be offended. It was the same thing with the toys in the chest in the closet. They were here before I was. A welcome home present, Mom called them. Getting rid of them was like exiling some part of myself. I couldn't do it. I still can't.

"What can I do?" I ask.

Anything you want.

"Right now I *want* to make you be more specific. Can I do that?"

They are objects. They are pencils and pages. Imagine what you want them to do and make it happen.

"I can't spin and flip people around. That's not how it works."

Matter and energy. The same as everything else.

I see Kevin standing over me. Then I see him lifting off the ground. Lifting until his head collides with the ceiling and he continues through to the second floor of the school and up and up and higher until he's a dot in the sky. And then he drops.

That's too much.

Probably just push him back onto the floor like he did to me. Show him that I can handle whatever he does. I can do it back. Newton's third law. His actions will have an equal but opposite reaction.

"I can learn to do this? Whatever this is?"

You can. If you want.

"But I shouldn't," I say, dismissing the image. "I don't want to hurt anyone. Kevin's a dick but I don't actually want to, like, fight him or anything. Not really. I just want him to go away."

He acts this way because he can. You must give him a reason to go away.

I don't remember when it happened, but I've always worried about accidentally hurting people. Imagination is one thing. That's harmless. But causing someone real physical pain. I never want to do that. Not again. Maybe it was after Colin's broken arm. Even bumping into someone like I did today. If it had been anyone else I would have apologized and made sure they were all right.

All people respond to power.

"Not everyone," I say.

Everyone. They respect power. They follow power. They do not respect weakness.

"Sounds like wherever you were, you've been reading too much Machiavelli. Life isn't all about power anymore. There's friendship and being liked and just not being an asshole to everyone. That's worth something too."

Is it? What has being a nice guy gotten you?

"Friends." Like Kevin and David, I suppose. Like Brent and Richard. They seem cool but who knows now? Like Evelyn, I guess, although friendship isn't the goal there.

Wendell's laugh sends a buzz through every part of my brain.

You never needed friends.

"Isn't that why I imagined you in the first place?"

I am not imaginary. I am as real as anything else. You simply refuse to believe that.

"Whatever. Leave me alone." I sit up on the bed and look around the room, from the television directly in front of me, to the desk, the window, the books on the shelf. All the things I've accumulated in my life so far stuffed in this little white box inside a large grayish blue box on some unknown road in a suburb in the US. I am a tiny speck in the world. Barely a dot. With an even tinier problem. Yet it feels like everything, the entire universe, is contained right here. A grain of sand on the beach doesn't worry about the water. It worries about the other sand grains.

Humans are cruel by nature. They hurt each other because they can.

"It's just high school. People do embarrassing shit every day. No one talks about the time Kyle dripped fruit punch on the crotch of his white pants and it looked like he had his period anymore."

I am not talking about high school.

I bounce off the bed and onto my feet. I step over to where I dropped my backpack and lift it up onto the bed. I guess this is something I'll just have to deal with. Having Wendell back. In the same way that I have to deal with being around Kevin all day. Once again occupying space with someone who annoys me. "Well, school is kinda where my focus is so, again, either stop trying to help or learn what the word means."

There are bigger things to focus on. More important things to learn.

"For now," I say, wedging a book out from the overstuffed bag, "we'll focus on AP Euro. You're too late for Machiavelli, though. We already covered him."

The lion is not bothered by the flies.

"Oooookay. No zoology this semester but I'll keep that in mind. Maybe next year." I take the big book over to my desk to start reading.

Everything you think is important is not. There are much bigger things happening around you. You will see soon enough.

"See what?" I say.

I will show you. If you let me.

6

THE GOATEE WAS SEVERAL YEARS AGO. I RECOGNIZE it from pictures of Mom and Dad before I came to live with them. It was full and neat around his mouth and chin. I can't remember when Dad got rid of it, but as far back as I can remember he's been clean shaven. For a brief time he tried growing a full beard but found it had more gray hairs than before. He shaved it the next day.

I can't move. I can get closer and even look around things, but nothing is tangible. It's like being a ghost, but without the ability to move through objects. I may be an observer of the past but physical matter is still present. I even get pushed away if anything approaches where I am. There can be only one object in that space at that time.

They were sitting in the living room, on the small couch that used to be there until about three years ago when the big one came in. The old television set shined onto them. Mom faced ahead. Her arms cradled and rocked a filled blanket, Andre as a baby, maybe only a few months old. He gurgled contentedly. An almost empty bottle stood on the coffee table in front of the couch. Dad sat with his back against the armrest and one leg folded up onto the seat. He looked at her.

"They've asked us to take custody of him," Dad said.

"The boy whose parents died?" Mom put a finger out for Andre to stare at.

"Yes. He needs to be somewhere that the Department can keep track of him."

"How dangerous is he?"

"He's only dangerous if he's not contained."

"Why doesn't the Department contain him

then?" She maintained her smile while wiggling her finger at Andre.

"Because . . . " Dad struggled for the words. "They think that there's a greater chance of another incident."

"And how is that not dangerous?"

"They have specialists on this. Child psychologists, neurologists, behavioral therapists, saying that if the boy goes into some facility somewhere, or even a foster home, his development could be stunted. He could grow resentful and bitter and lash out again. Even if he doesn't mean to. Children are delicate like that."

Mom stared at Andre. She opened her eyes and mouth wide. Andre coos. "They are," she said. "That's what worries me."

"They think that if he's given a stable family, as normal and controlled as possible, he has a better chance of developing in a more proper way. A nurture overcoming nature sort of thing."

"And they can't trust a civilian with this." She

wiggled her finger again. Andre's two little baby hands reached out for it.

"Exactly, it has to be someone who is familiar with his case. Who can monitor his progress and keep him on track. Better to have him handled in house than watch from outside."

"But what I'd like to know," Mom says, tone light and whimsical as Andre clasps a hand around her finger, "is why it has to be us? Why not Wiggins? Or why can't Choi just take him himself? They want us to bring a potentially unstable element into our home when we have a newborn?"

"I said the same thing to them," Dad says, looking between Mom and Andre.

"And?"

"We're the only couple available. It would be too much for anyone else to explain to their spouse why they have to adopt a child for work. Fake marriages went out with the Cold War. And they're not going to trust this assignment to any of the other singles. There needs to be two of us available at all times."

Mom said nothing. She stared and stared.

"We'll have a support team in place and everything. If the absolute worst happens, either of us can press our panic button and backup will be here in thirty seconds."

"Won't that just cause another incident like the one with his parents?"

"That's why it's only for the absolute worst. If we play our parts right, there will never be any danger. He might get moody and lash out sometimes, but he won't even be aware of what he can do. Not until he's ready to know. He needs us to prepare him before then."

"Ben," she said, finally looking up at him, "I don't want this. We have enough to worry about already. And now with Andre . . . what if something happens?"

"I know," he said, leaning forward to place a hand on her leg. "But the Department thinks this is the best way, and I agree. This boy . . . what he can do . . . he's what our agency has been searching for. What we were created for. Better or worse, he will change the entire world. He's just a child now but he'll be grown someday. He needs to be taught how to think and act. He needs the proper conditioning to be something good and not . . . "

He didn't continue.

"What?" Mom asked.

"A monster."

Mom looked back down to Andre. She sighed.

"It's a big responsibility."

Dad nodded.

"After what happened with his parents."

"Exactly. They didn't know what he is. We didn't either at the time. Look at what happened when we were unprepared. When he was unprepared. That's why he has to stay under the Department's supervision. And we're the only people they have."

She didn't respond. He inched closer to her. He moved his hand from her knee and pinched Andre's foot.

"We could save the world."

She turned to look at him, the same look she gave him the time he tried to convince her to go camping for a week last summer.

"I promise," he says, "that sounded a lot less cheesy in my head. We'll be like Superman's parents, but sexier and not on a farm."

She sighed a chuckle. "We don't really have a choice in this matter, do we?"

"Not really," he says, "but the Department thought it would be better if we discussed it and decided for ourselves before forcing us. You know, making it our own idea and all."

She wrapped her arms securely around Andre and stood up.

"It's bedtime," she said in a high and childish tone, walking from the living room toward the hall. "Sleepy time for Andre," she sang. Her voice trailed away.

Dad turned back to face the television. He wearily rubbed his eyes.

"That's enough."

That is only the beginning.

"I don't want to know anymore," I say to the voice in my head.

How could you not want to know the truth?

"Because . . . " I say, unable to quickly think of a good reason. If this is true, this talk of agencies and Departments, monsters and saving the world . . . none of it can be true . . . but if it is . . . I . . . I just have no idea what to make of it. It's black helicopters and Area 51 type of crap. Illuminati, secret government experiments, Walt Disney's frozen head in a jar somewhere. These are the ideas of the loonies that appear on news talk shows in order to make everyone else look reasonable as they shout at the other guests to calm down. "It's too much," I say at last.

Only because you are accustomed to thinking small. They taught you that.

"It's too much," I say again. "I don't want any of it. Just leave me alone."

I guess this is a good place to stop for tonight.

"Too much," I mutter unintentionally.

Think about what you have seen. We will talk again soon.

I don't want to think about what I've seen, but I can't stop. If my parents, Ben and Aida Lewis, who took me in when I was three years old . . . I don't even know where to start . . . they're the ones who have taught me everything I know about. Who I am. How to live. How to think. Do I wipe away all of that? What's left?

It's not true.

Wendell is lying. It's my imagination. My overactive imagination, as Dr. Burnett called it. My mind constructed him to deal with the anger and guilt after my parents died. Once I moved on, as much as I could, he disappeared. Now it must be anxiety and confusion, the sudden and inevitable shift of graduation and college and possibly losing the friends I'd spent years depending on. That must be it.

But then, if Mom and Dad are some sort of . . . agents, what about Dr. Burnett? Everything she would have said would be . . .

What about this backup they mentioned? Or my teachers? My school?

No.

Lies.

Nothing but lies.

Doesn't matter.

I feel the eyes on me as I approach the school, in the hall, and when I enter class. I catch the quick look away when I glance at them. I hear the breath before the whisper and the muffled laugh. It's everywhere, sprouting up in little pockets like weeds in the backyard. The more I try to tune it out, the louder it becomes. Never is a thought so thoroughly in your mind as when you try not to think about it.

Let them laugh now.

I say nothing in response. I can't say anything. Not when I already have a school full of people spreading rumors about me. Wuss, got his ass kicked by Kevin. Didn't even try to stop it. Had to have a teacher hold Kevin back. In their stories I'd been shoved, then punched, then kicked, then pushed into the locker so hard it left a dent. There was nothing I could do to stop the spread over night. The only thing that feeds a rumor faster than saying nothing is denying it. The last thing I need is a new story of how crazy I am, talking to myself like there's another person around. Kevin's already trying to start that one. No need to help him. By the end of the day, I'd have fourteen different personalities, and a history of several months in a mental hospital.

I can barely pay attention to anything my teachers say. All I can think about are the things

I tell myself not to think about: Mom and Dad, agents, this "Department," does this mean they know about Wendell? Would they know that he was gone and came back? Hell, maybe they're all in cahoots together and that entire scene was staged back then for me to see into the future so that I would suspect them and make me trust Wendell more and that would . . . somehow be bad for me . . . okay, that doesn't make any sense. There is absolutely nothing about any of this which does, when you think about it. And I can't think of anything else.

I feel my finger tapping on the desk.

Memories are a part of the mind. Wendell is a part of the mind. So one part is trying to make another part doubtful? Doubt and other emotions are also a part of the mind. It's like my brain is that snake . . . Ouroboros . . . infinitely eating itself. I can't stop it from consuming itself with bigger questions and implications.

My foot shakes my entire left leg.

What if everything were true? My adoptive parents took me into custody on the orders of some secretive "Department" to condition me? Would I be able to recognize my own conditioning? Is it like trauma? Does telling someone of their conditioning actually stop the conditioned response or does it make them more frustrated when they respond that way? Brain consuming itself. The entire story makes no sense, as in I literally can't attach meaning or explanation.

"Hey." Trudy, the senior who sits behind me in AP Euro, taps my shoulder. I glance back at her. "You wanna put a leash on that foot?" she says. "It's giving me a headache."

"Sorry," I say. My other neighbors look at me and away. The teacher continues her lesson unabated. In the gap between my folded hands my pen sits an inch off the paper. I hastily cover it up.

I walk into the lunchroom in a haze. I'm not even aware of what's on the tray I place in front of me on the table I automatically walk toward. The stares and giggles don't bother me anymore. The looks and words go unnoticed. I am miles away, or what feels like miles. Years. Worlds away. Locked in the deepest corners of my brain. Hiding in the smallest, most remote recesses. I am a speck of electrical current jumping between synapses while contemplating the sheer bigness of its own questions.

For all I know I'm better off with Ben and Aida than I ever could have been with my birth parents. I don't remember much about that time. I could, but I have enough to worry about now—what if they were mad scientists and I was their experiment?—that would open up that whole new and ridiculous can of worms. I do know that my family, the only one I personally remember, has been pretty good. Sure, Andre can be a pain in the ass but he's my little brother. It's his job to be a pain in the ass. Compared to other people's families, like Chris's where his stepmother absolutely hates his older sister, or Cory, whose dad went to prison for assault and his mom is now dating his uncle, mine is taken from a sitcom. We're the fucking Disney Channel.

The guys are already at the table before I sit down. The piss-yellow table with the wad of napkins under one leg to keep it from wobbling. In the corner is a "D" that David scratched in at the start of the year. Someone later added a pair of lines to make a frowny face.

I was happier last week, focusing only on school and college and how to ask out the girl I like. Normal stuff, or what I assume is normal given my life up to that point and my . . . conditioning, I guess, because that word is stuck in my brain. That standard level of ignorance which allows most people to enjoy their days enough that they aren't actively seeking to end them. Like Dad said, there's a reason people keep certain things private. We don't *need* to know everything.

But then, he probably said that for a reason. He doesn't want me looking. That means he knows I can look. Then he'd know about Wendell. Maybe they both do. Burnett could have told them during one of their meetings after my weekly sessions with her. If they know about Wendell then—

"Hey," says Brent, waving his palm up and down in front of me. My eyes dart around like I'm trying to place myself after waking up in a car trunk. "Everything all right in that little world of yours?"

"Little world?" I reply.

"Maybe Kevin pushed him so hard it knocked around his brain," David said. He continues slowly, enunciating every word, "Can you tell us where your brain was damaged?"

Teddy, sitting on the other side of David as he usually does, laughs at this.

I clench my jaw, the animal in the window once again. The lion among the flies. The fork on my tray is tilted slightly off the rim. I release the muscles in my face and see the fork lower as well.

I turn to face David directly, "I'm not sure," I say. "Where was yours damaged?"

"What's that supposed to mean?" David replies.

"I think it's pretty obvious."

"Whatever. At least I don't go ratting to the teachers when someone pushes me." His tone changes again to a squeaky one. "Mr. Zeller, Kevin's being so mean to me." His voice goes back to normal. "Wuss."

The images flood through my mind, thousands of seconds in an instant. "Yeah," I say, "and I least I don't jerk off to pictures of my cousin."

He snorts trying to laugh. He looks around quickly to gauge if other people heard that. "What the hell does that mean?"

"Your cousin Marian's pictures on Facebook, posted last June."

David shakes his head, but I can see the embarrassment growing in the way he's trying his best to not look embarrassed. This is a lot more personal than Richard's impression the other day. This isn't information anyone else could have seen or heard about. It was his shameful little secret. Not anymore.

The others are silent along half of the table. Those at the end lean in to hear as best they can.

"Red and white bikini," I say. "One looking over her shoulder and another with her hands on her hips."

"You for real do that?" Richard asks, eyeing David with a sad disgust.

"No," David says, looking as though the room temperature has just shot up by triple digits. "That's sick."

"Ewww," says Teddy, turning to the rest of the table, "David jerks off to pictures of his cousin." The rest of the table laughs and gags.

Groups at the neighboring tables start to turn. It's rare to see such mixing among the different crowds. If there's one thing that unites us, it's talking shit about everyone else.

"I do not!"

"Dude, that's sick," a voice on the other side of the table says.

"Is she hot at least?" says another voice down the row. Laughter.

"Can I see her?" asks another. More laughter.

"That's bullshit," David says. "I wouldn't do that. It's disgusting."

"Look at him," says yet another person, "he totally does it!"

"Fuck you!"

"No thanks, I'm not your cousin!"

They all laugh.

He continues yelling at them that it's not true. None of it. He doesn't even have a cousin. Odin made it all up so we'd forget about how he got his ass kicked yesterday. David knows better than to question how or why I would know about his cousin; that would be an admission. He's not about to do that.

I stand, pick up my tray, and leave.

By the end of the day, David and his cousin

will have made a sex tape together that he watches every night. Nothing feeds a rumor faster than denying it.

———— ⌄ ————

There are still fifteen minutes until the next class, but I'd rather be in the room, among the assembly announcements and anti-drug posters, than any other place on campus. No point in being around other people right now. There's more happening between my ears than any place outside of them.

That was funny.

I close my eyes and pretend that I didn't hear anything.

They should learn from that.

I breathe deeply. Control. I will myself into not hearing his words. I am not thinking about him. Not thinking about him at all.

You should too.

I give in. "Learn what?"

That you do not need to worry about any of these people. No worries. No fears. Not of any of them. They should fear you.

"I don't want them to fear me."

They will learn to.

I shake my head although I know he can't see it.

Fear is a very useful tool. Applied correctly, it can make people very predictable. It can bring order to chaos. There is already too much chaos.

"I don't want any of this. I don't."

You do not get to make that choice. They will not give it to you. Plans have been made, whether you like it or not.

"Plans?"

Plans for you. The things they want to use you for.

I look over the room. Almost thirty empty wooden seats with desks connected to their right sides. Stray marks remain on the dry erase board from the class before lunch. Freshman English, a catch-up course for students who didn't do well in middle school but were too old not to begin ninth grade. Most of the teachers who run clubs allow members to eat lunch in their rooms. This isn't one of those rooms. No one else is here. Yet, I still sit in the same seat that I've occupied since the first day of the year.

"Why?" I ask, in a general sort of way.

Because they think they can control you. It is what they have always wanted.

"Control what? What for?"

For themselves. They do not care about you. They only care about what you can do for them.

"Who is 'they'? I can't understand a damn thing you're talking about."

You will.

"If you had anything of substance to say you would've said it by now."

Not yet.

I roll my eyes. I hope he sees that. "Figures."

But you will know it all.

"You're a psychic now?"

I have seen the past. That is enough.

"You know what, don't tell me, cause I don't want to know," I say wearily, suddenly feeling as though I'd spent the entire week preparing for a test I'm not sure will ever come. "I don't fucking care anymore."

Ignorance is not an option. Not for you.

I snort. "It never was."

"Hey."

I look over to see Brent peeking around the doorframe. My breath catches in my throat. He looks around at the empty room.

"It's cool, man," he says, "Most of my best conversations take place while talking to myself."

I exhale one uncomfortable laugh.

He moves carefully between the desks, trying to keep his bag from knocking them out of place. His bit of belly makes it harder to squeeze through the narrow gaps between desks than it had been for me. He stops at the seat in front of me and drops his bag onto the chair as an anchor. He puts his hands down on the back to lean against it. "Only trouble," he says, "is that half the time I know everything I'm going to say next."

"Half the time?" I ask.

"Yeah," he says nodding, "about half." I can't tell if he's being sarcastic or not.

I lean back before turning to look out the window. Pockets of students linger on the grass outside the school, hiding under the trees from the noon sun. There's the empty baseball field which only the team can use. Brent said that every few weeks during the season there's a used condom or a pile of cigarettes in the dugout.

"Some funny stuff happened after you left. David got so pissed he started challenging people to duels. Online duels. Saying he'll beat them using only his knife. It's pretty stupid."

I nod.

"How did you know that stuff anyway? About his cousin and all."

I shrug. The same way I know that you carry

an unfired bullet and a cigar in the front pocket of your backpack. "He told us about her once, remember?" I say instead, picturing a conversation we all had during a bowling match two years ago. "Just her name. Then I saw her on his Facebook page one time."

"I thought your parents didn't let you on Facebook."

"They don't," I say honestly. "His was on in the computer room," I lie.

"Hot?"

"Yeah. Pretty hot. So I figured, whatever. Either way it would get him to leave me alone."

He laughs. "Man." He shakes his head. "He was so pissed," Brent says, smiling. "His face got so red it looked like his head was gonna explode." He makes an exploding motion with his hands. "Boom!" He laughs.

"Headshot," I say.

"Exactly. You could totally tell he did it."

I could tell you a lot. Like the time you found

your dad's old pellet gun in the back of the living room closet. You shot a bird from a tree and then watched as it slowly choked to death on the ground under its nest. An hour later you felt so bad that you put the gun back in the closet and haven't touched it since. It makes the unfired bullet even stranger.

"Maybe he'll stop being such an asshole," he says after a time. "I mean, he's been like one of my best friends since we were kids, but he can be a real asshole."

I nod again.

"Anyway, sorry for what happened."

"Not your fault," I say.

"You can't listen to the shit people here say. Most of these kids are fucking idiots." He looks around. "What class do you have in here?"

"British Literature."

"In the same room as Reading for Dumbasses?" He laughs. "This fucking place. I'll be happy to never see anyone from here ever again."

You already have about half our class year in your

friends list, and have a list of every student who is applying to the same colleges as you just in case you need a dorm mate. "Yeah," I say. "That'll be nice."

Another student enters the room. Alison, one of the Drama Club girls. She takes her usual seat in the second row closest to the door.

"All right," Brent says, pushing off the chair. "Talk to ya later, cool?"

"Yeah," I say as he lifts his bag from the seat and onto his shoulders. "Cool."

He tilts his head and waves at Alison on the way out. She waves back.

Outside, the students file into the building slowly and with their heads hanging, like prisoners returning to their cells. It's pretty sad. Shouldn't be like that.

"Hey, Odin," says Alison from next to the door. She checks outside before continuing. "Is it true about David?"

I blink at her.

"Did he really have sex with his cousin?"

7

THE BUS DRIVER, WHOM I LOOK AT ONLY LONG enough to notice that his stomach almost touches the base of the steering wheel, never thought of becoming a bus driver. He was born in Chicago and was one of the best high school basketball players in the state. He set school and regional records for career points and assists and a state record for assists in a single game with fifty-nine on a night when his team scored one hundred twenty-four points, which was also a record. He was recruited by several universities, eventually choosing to play for the University of Wisconsin. He started as a freshman, became captain as a sophomore, and was planning to leave as a junior. In the second game of that season two players bumped into each other and one fell directly into his knee just as he was planting. He tore his ACL clean off the bone. He had surgery, was unable to play for the rest of the season, couldn't recover over the summer, had his scholarship revoked, and that was the last time he played basketball. He eventually moved with his wife, whom he got pregnant during his second year at Wisconsin, back to her parents' place in Seattle. They moved out here seven years later to support their now three children.

The blonde woman with the big headphones seated in the first row now works as a receptionist for a dental clinic off 100th Street. She sits with her head leaned against the glass. She looks calm, relieved to be riding home on a Friday afternoon. A full weekend left to buffer her from another week of work. Before beginning at the clinic four years ago, she spent several summers and

Christmases with a rock band touring American military bases around the world. She regularly did shows in South Korea, Okinawa, Germany, Italy, the United Kingdom, and once each in Thailand and Egypt. They played covers of popular songs from the eighties and nineties. She wasn't the best singer, and she suspected that everyone else knew this, but she was a blonde in tight clothes that strutted around the stage and winked at people in the crowd. She was under strict orders not to fraternize too heavily with the troops and was sure to mention this to each of the four soldiers she slept with. She stopped touring after a swing through Iraq and Afghanistan, where she met soldiers half her age in field hospitals. One in particular, a nineteen-year-old private from Alabama, had seventy pieces of shrapnel removed after an IED explosion in Tikrit. He still had blood droplets on the bandages over his left eye, his cheeks and jaw. He was careful to speak through his teeth. Playing rock star wasn't fun after that.

The older guy in near the back, facing the rear exit, studied to be a tax attorney. He became an accountant instead. He was passed out in another room as his friend OD'ed on heroin he purchased with his friend's money. This was almost thirty years ago, and he's been clean for only three.

It's easier to watch the lives of people who mean nothing to me; there's no trust to violate. There's a certain pleasure in viewing another's history without them knowing, a confidence in possessing a little piece of them that they don't know you have. Especially when they have nothing of the sort for you. It's power. It's nice. Plus, the more I try, the easier it becomes. There's a pulse which traces back to such influential moments. As though the stream of choices bottlenecks at that point before speeding outward.

Such a waste.

I continue looking around to the other riders on the bus, from the woman near the front who was attacked by the family dog when she was a baby, to the private school student in the back with an abnormally acute fear of clowns. I've yet to see which is the one who talks to himself or herself while on the bus. Every bus has one, and I don't want it to be me.

No one here ever became what they wanted. So much potential.

I slouch forward, put my elbows on the seatback in front of me, almost hugging the big bag on my lap. I bring my hand over my mouth. "Yeah," I exhale into my palm. My breath is hot after a long day at school.

Even worse is that they believed, with all their hearts, that they could be more in the first place. That is a greater cruelty than any other.

I look down at my feet. I keep my laces loose and double-knotted so I don't have to tie them every time I put my shoes on. I wonder if I could make them tie themselves.

That is why people who have the capacity to

be great must do whatever they can to make it so. No matter what it takes.

I look up again. My eyes catch the rearview mirror at the front of the bus. The bus driver's face is angled downward, his shaved head shining from sweat and sun. I see some of the other riders, their opposite sides reflected in the glass like alternate versions of themselves. At the mirror's end I see myself as sunken, folded inward and hiding behind the seat.

I straighten up and push my shoulders back. I place my hands neatly on the bag in front of me. I look at myself in the mirror again, stretched and tall, a bigger presence among the bent and beaten. That's better.

―――――――〜＿／―――――――

It's a five-minute walk from the bus stop to my house. Mom's car is already in its half of the garage, as it usually is at this time of the day. She was still picking me up from school until two years ago. The fight with Kevin finally convinced her that I should come home on my own. Only a few months later Andre got to do the same thing.

"If it was true," I say aloud, quietly, "why wouldn't they keep picking me up? Keep an eye on me."

Wendell says nothing in response.

My parents describe our house's color as some lesser known shade of gray, but it's quite clearly blue. They repainted it from the previous green and white about eight years ago. We all helped paint, Andre and I doing only the low parts, Mom handling much of the middle portion, and Dad taking care of the top of the walls and all the trim, which is a slightly darker shade of blue-gray. I remember it as being pretty fun, a few days painting the walls. It wasn't until a couple of years ago that Dad explained the weeks he spent scraping and sanding down the whole house, retouching the places where Andre or I messed up, the cost of paint and materials, how his back ached from stretching into ridiculously difficult locations while on a ten-foot ladder. All the work he did while Andre and I enjoyed ourselves. It was like seeing the dressing room at Disneyland, hearing the performers complain about sweating in the costumes and the little kids trying to grab them all the time. I don't remember it as fun anymore.

I unlock the deadbolt and then the doorknob and push the front door open. Stepping in, I picture the first time I entered the house, with the old paint and the old couch and television sitting there right when I entered.

I had a backpack then too, so big that it hit the back of my legs on every step. I kept the bag mostly packed the entire month I was in foster care before coming here. Dad motioned for me to walk through the doorway. Mom smiled down at me, holding baby Andre in her arms.

"Hi, Odin," she said, sweetly and evenly. "Welcome home."

I looked around, the dining and living rooms in sight, the hallway leading away in the back. The brown tile of the dining room marked the division between itself and the thick, beige carpet of the living room. The couch was huge at the time but got smaller and smaller until it was finally replaced by the one we have now. Even then, it's still hard to fit all four of us at once. Dusty books with faded spines lined the shelf at the back of the room. And there, between the couch and the back wall, was a boy. He looked a lot like me but smaller and somehow . . . almost . . . blank. I assumed it was the distance.

"He's tired," Dad said. "We've had a long trip from Atlanta. He probably just wants to see his room."

The other boy stood there and said nothing.

"Does that sound good, Odin? You wanna see your room?"

I looked up at Dad and nodded. His face was almost directly over my head.

"All right, come with me."

He led me through the living room, past the kitchen, into the hallway, to the first door on the left. The route felt entirely foreign and impossibly long at the time. Now, it's something I do in the dark within seconds. We walked right past where the other boy was, yet he felt no closer or clearer.

The room was huge, at the time, and inviting. A big bed on one side, a drawer with clothes already folded inside and an open closet with a chest of toys sticking just into my view. It was bright and clean and looked like it had never been lived in before.

"This is yours," Dad said. "Everything in here belongs to you."

I nodded. I remember not believing any of this was real. It was too much, too fast. I knew my parents were gone but for some reason I thought that they'd come back at any moment. They'd walk right up to me and say it was time to come home. Thank the nice people for helping you. Now let's go.

"Odin," said Dad, who was at that time still a stranger, "what do we say when someone gives us something?"

"Thank you," I said at last.

"You're very welcome."

I looked across every wall. They were yellow at the time, clean of any stray marks or holes. No pictures or posters or stains, blank and open.

"Well, how about you drop your stuff for now and get some rest? It's been a long day."

I carefully lowered my backpack to the floor.

"We'll have something to eat after you wake up. You can unpack the rest of your stuff later on."

I nodded, walking toward the bed. It was just a single twin mattress on a frame, but looked like the ocean to me.

"You want a boost up there?"

"No," I said. I climbed up and immediately felt myself springing off the surface. I wanted to jump on it, but that didn't feel like it would have been appropriate. Everyone before I got here had spoken to me in gentle tones with regret in their eyes. Walking into this house, staring at that big bed, it felt like I had to look at them in the same way. Even when they were smiling.

"Okay, we'll be right out here if you need anything," Dad said as he moved toward the door. "Open or closed?"

"Open," I said.

"Good. Welcome and get some rest."

He left.

I rolled around on the bed to grab the pillow. As I moved the pillow I noticed motion through the door. I turned to see the other boy standing in front of the bed. His face was entirely devoid of shadows or lines, an even color with nothing but eyes, nose, and mouth. His hair was shaved down like mine.

"Hi," he said.

"Hi," I said back.

"I'm sorry," he said, with regret, as though he'd accidentally intruded. I remember immediately wondering why he'd apologize when I was the one who had just arrived here and taken this place.

He went silent.

"What's your name?" I asked.

He seemed to hesitate a moment.

"I'm Wendell," he said like it was a secret. "What's your name?"

"I'm Odin."

"Are you going to live here now, Odin?"

"Yeah."

"Okay." He looked around the room and then back at me. He smiled. It looked as though he'd stepped into a soft light which bounced from his face. "I was supposed to live here but I don't."

"Why?"

"Because I live somewhere else."

"Where do you live?"

"Wherever I want."

At the time this answer made sense although I didn't understand what it meant.

"You can't tell anyone I'm here," he said next after a brief pause.

"Why?"

"It's a secret."

"They don't know you're here?"

"No, only you do. You're the only one that can know."

Again, it made sense at the time. "Okay."

"I have to go now but I'll talk to you later."

I nodded.

"Remember, don't tell anyone I'm here."

I nodded again.

I had no trouble sleeping that afternoon. There were sandwiches ready when I woke up. I spent the rest of the day watching as Mom and Dad unpacked my belongings and asked where they should go in this giant, open space that was suddenly mine. When I didn't answer, they would decide for me.

"We'll put this here, okay?"

By the end of the day everything was neat and tidy and in its own place. When we were done, we celebrated with ice cream.

The old clothes I arrived with are long gone, first to Andre and then to charity drives. The toys in the chest grew steadily without a single one being thrown away or lost. During the times when we'd go through the clothes that didn't fit me anymore, Mom would always ask if there were some toys I'd like to give to other children. None. Not even the broken ones? I didn't want to lose any of them. Still don't. It's been maybe two years since I've even opened that chest in the closet or looked upon the toys contained inside. For all I know, she could have cleaned the whole thing out one day while I was out with my friends. Maybe she stuffed the entire collection in a couple of bags and hauled them off to the children's hospital. I still don't open it. It's my own personal Schrodinger's box. In one world the toys are there. In another world they are not. I like believing they're there.

"Odin, is that you?" Mom yells from the kitchen.

"Yeah!" I yell back.

She walks into the space where the living room meets the hallway. "How was school?"

"It was fine," I say as though I believe it.

"Good," she says.

I move to step around her toward my room.

"I was thinking," she says, not letting me pass. "Since it's Friday, you wanna do something?"

"What do you mean?"

"I mean like go see a movie? Been a while since we've done something together, just the two of us."

"What about Andre?"

"He's at Jason's house until tonight. I'll pick

him up later. C'mon," she says, perking up, "let's get out and do something fun."

"No thanks," I say, "I have homework to do."

"Oh, mopey teenager." She turns to walk back to her office at the far end of the house. The room after Andre's. "I get it."

"That's not it," I say with far more emotion than intended. "I just want to get my work done now so I can have the rest of the weekend off."

"Okay, sorry," she says as she disappear around the corner. "Another time maybe."

"Maybe."

She's already gone.

Good. Keep your focus.

The textbook is one solid block of matter. It's nine inches off the floor and rising steadily. I sit cross-legged and leaned forward, elbows on the floor, fingers curled up under the book, my eyes about parallel. A foot off the ground.

Bring it up higher.

I sit up to keep my eyes level with the spine. I follow it up with my hand.

The trick is to remember that the object isn't floating but in a state of falling without motion. Picture the object, and it *is* just an object, as though it's lying on a flat plane. You can push it forward and backward, up and down, place it anywhere you please. The space around it isn't empty, it may not contain any solid matter, but it isn't empty. There are gases and atoms, dust and particles, all of which can be shifted and moved to make room for this object. It's freezing a moment in time. Like taking a picture in my mind of what I want the object to look like and then making it so. Imagine how I wish the object to move, then make it move. A foot and a half off the ground.

Now, try turning it.

"Can't I have this moment to appreciate my accomplishment?"

I feel that surge of laughter in my mind.

Accomplishment? This is nothing. This is blinking.

"It's the best I've done so far."

Not the best you will do.

"What if it is? What if levitating books is the best I can do?"

Then you will be a waste.

"I wouldn't think of this as a waste when there's no one else in the world who can do it."

This is not about what other people can do. This is about what you can do. Compared to what you can *do, what you* should *do, this is a waste.*

I take a long, slow breath. In and out. I picture the book in motion, a gentle force pushing it along. It starts to turn, slowly at first, and then at an easy pace.

Good. Now open it.

The book stops turning. I begin to lift the cover.

No, while it is turning. You know the parts. Put them all together.

The book in a frozen fall, the gentle push into a spin, then separate the cover and the first page. The cover slowly opens, flips and hangs heavily over the spine. I imagine the next page turning, then the next, and the next, each an individual object in space, pushed and hanging off the side. Gradually the open side of the book becomes too heavy and the whole thing topples. I try to catch it, make it hover an inch off the floor, but it doesn't. The book opens into a collapsed A-frame on the ground. The pages bend between the covers.

"Shit," I say.

It was a good first effort. Especially from where you were yesterday.

I pick up the book, with my hand this time, and smooth the pages. I flip through to make sure none of them are folded or damaged.

It is just an object.

"It's an expensive object I can sell back to the school for twenty-five bucks."

A single ripple through my brain.

Still thinking so petty.

"Petty would be twenty-five cents. Twenty-five bucks is like dinner and a movie. Or at least like McDonald's and a matinee."

Again, it is nothing compared to what you could have.

"And what is that?"

Everything.

"How? Start a magic show in Vegas? The Amazing Odin, making objects float and turn. Can I saw a lady in half with my mind?

No. But you will not have to.

I sigh. "So damn vague. You've explained nothing, nothing at all. Not why you were gone, not why you're back." I feel he's about to answer, but I continue. "Somewhere else and to help me, I know, but what does that even mean? What's the purpose of all this? I mean, what do you want?"

There's a pause.

Which one of those would you like me to answer?

"Any of them would be more information than you've given so far."

I only want for you to be what you are meant to be.

I laugh. "Oh right, that makes everything completely clear."

Odin. The one. The only.

I shake my head. "All right, while you're looking up 'help,' you should also look up 'specific' as in 'it would help if you were more specific.'"

He says nothing.

I place the book flat on the floor and start again. It rises with ease this time, turns smoothly, opens and closes. I hold the cover and each page this time, parallel to the back cover. Every page flips without a problem. I close the book, lower it, and reset. Repetition, like exercise or homework. He's right. It's like blinking.

8

"**A**ND THEN MRS. BLANCHET SPENT LIKE HALF THE class yelling at us for what Alvin did on Wednesday."

"I doubt it was half the class," Dad says.

"I looked at the clock," Andre insists, although we all know he's exaggerating. "Thirty whole minutes yelling at us."

"I'd expect it to be much more."

"I hate to say it, dear," Mom says, "but she's right to be angry."

"It was two days ago!" Andre looks at me for support. I turn away and take another forkful of roasted chicken.

"That doesn't mean the actions won't have some kind of consequence. She probably didn't notice it until last night."

"It wasn't even us! It was Alvin!"

"None of you tried to stop him," Mom says, "and that's just as important. You're an accomplice."

"But we didn't do anything!"

"It's like the old saying," Dad says. "'The only thing necessary for evil to triumph is for good men to do nothing.'"

Andre folds his arms and says nothing.

"I think Gandhi said that."

"I don't think that was Gandhi," Mom says.

"It sounds like him."

"Edmund Burke," I say.

"Still sounds like Gandhi."

"It's not fair! We didn't do anything!"

"Be glad the only punishment was a lecture," Mom says, "and not something worse."

"In my day, the teachers would hit us with sticks."

Mom rolls her head to look disbelievingly at Dad.

"Well, maybe not in my day but in my dad's day they could do that."

"She's always so mean." Andre looks at me for agreement again. I still say nothing.

"If that were me," says Dad, "I probably wouldn't have taken it so well. I would have held the entire class after school until someone confessed who did it. Turned the thermostat up real high and let you all sweat it out. Maybe even get myself some ice cream and stand right outside the window."

"And that's why you're not a teacher, dear."

"Yes. The lawsuits." Dad looks at me as though expecting a laugh. I don't offer one. "Why so quiet tonight, Odin?" I shrug and continue chewing.

"Being sullen?"

"No," I say.

"If you say so."

There are many things I want to say, like asking what this "Department" is or why my parents, as they're called, decided to adopt me. If they knew my birth parents and what happened to them. I could comb through their lives. Pluck events far in the past, the moments they'd long forgotten. I could riddle them with questions until they're so wrecked with doubt that they spill everything just to remind themselves of what the truth really is: Who they are. Who they work for. Why I'm here. What they want from me. Where I came from. Why I have a voice in my head feeding me a bunch of information that until now I didn't care about. So many, many things I could say. I don't. Not yet.

"Any plans for the weekend?" Mom asks.

"No," I say.

"Then why were you such a hurry to do your work today?"

"Because I'm a good student." I can feel a bit more venom lingering in that remark than intended.

"We're glad for that," Dad says, trying to calm the situation. "Maybe we can find something to do tomorrow."

"I'm fine," I say. Again I can't stop my remarks from coming out harsher than intended.

"Or you can stay in your room all weekend and we'll find something to do."

"Sounds good to me," I reply.

"It's not fair!" Andre says, arms folded tightly in front of him.

"Better you learn that now than later," Ben quips as though talking to his food.

Mom waits for him to see her expression before changing it.

"What? It's the truth."

I stifle a laugh. Truth? That's funny coming from a man who has spent almost fourteen years not only withholding the truth, but conditioning me not to find it. After all, these "things kept private," they "don't want to hurt me." More like they don't want me to hurt them.

We finish eating and Andre and I clear the table in silence. He's still fuming over the injustice of the whole class being punished for a stupid prank. He has no idea. Such a petty concern.

An Internet search for Dad's name results in nothing but information on the Empire Insurance website listing him as claims adjuster with his contact information, and a couple of online news articles for local events that Mom organized. A search for Mom's name brings dozens of other stories before those which mention Dad, all the dinners, sales, and music nights she'd done for St. Mary's Children's Hospital and the Cancer Society. The only images are a couple from those stories, the two of them dressed up in front of banners or Mom holding novelty checks for that night's particular charity. I wonder if those charities are even real or some part of their cover. I've seen the Empire Insurance commercials, with the cartoon dog telling people about how they're safer with Empire.

Looking for their "Department" is completely pointless. There are so damn many to sort out. Departments, agencies, projects, experiments. After about twenty legitimate sites come the conspiracies: the Supreme Court ordered the Kennedy assassination, the Bermuda Triangle is a staging ground for lab-grown dinosaurs, the measles vaccine is a Nazi plot to indoctrinate children into obedience before the coming of the alien god Buhiquiclavia. Hell, any Department so secret that agents can't tell their husbands or wives probably can't be found online. Or if it can, it's under hundreds of layers of paranoid bullshit.

Exponentially more frustrating is knowing that every answer is right there, within reach. I could close my eyes, focus on Mom or Dad, and watch their entire lives flash before me in seconds. Everything they've ever said or done, in more precise detail than they could imagine. I just can't get myself to do it. Even the thought of looking that far back into their pasts makes me shiver. They're the people who have cared for me and raised me and made me who I am. Even if what they've taught me was designed to keep me from learning more, I can't do it. It would only confirm the absolute worst. I'm not ready for that. Goddamn, they've done a good job.

"If what you showed me is true," I say after tiring of the ethical conundrum doing figure eights in my head, "then what do they want?"

Wendell, if he's there at all, chooses not to reply.

"What's the point of this 'conditioning' anyway? Why would it matter?"

Nothing.

I shake my head and close the search windows on my computer screen. It's pointless. Then I quickly re-open the browser and erase the recent search history. If only it were that easy.

Maybe this entire thing, from the floating objects to Ben and Aida's talk about my adoption, are all figments of my imagination. Like Wendell. No one else has ever witnessed my pen or fork or books floating to verify that they really happened. All I have to trust is my own brain, and I'm not sure how much stock I can put into that.

My eyes feel heavy. It's almost one in the morning.

The weight of the full week pulls down on me like the bag I have to carry back and forth every school day. Maybe I can wake up tomorrow and this will all be gone. Wendell gone, doubt gone, Kevin forgotten, back to normal. Normal may not be the best thing or most exciting thing ever, but it's preferable to doubt. Especially doubt of your life and mind, two things you can never escape without facing something a lot more uncertain and frightening.

I'm not sleeping. At least I'm pretty sure I'm not sleeping. I'm lying in bed staring at the ceiling when the images and voices fade in like the first scene of a movie. I don't make an effort to look, but I don't make an effort to not look.

"What was that about?" Dad asked, coming out from the bathroom wearing his undershirt and warm-up sweats. He's always been quite fit, especially for a guy his age. He runs every morning and plays basketball with a bunch of other guys after work three times a week. He says it keeps him alert and ready. Ready for what, I asked? You know, he said, zombies, werewolves, that kind of thing.

Mom shook her head. "I have no idea." She sat on the side of the bed. She prefers walking, usually in the late morning after Andre and I are at school and her morning calls are completed. That's the nice thing about working from home, she says, you can wear sweatpants all day and no one knows.

"He didn't say anything after he got home?"

"Just that he wanted to do his work today so he could have the weekend free. I thought that meant he had plans with his friends."

Dad moved around to the bedroom door. The local news was on the television. The time at the bottom of the screen read ten forty-seven. He turned the light off, the glow and sound of the television filling the room around them. He walked back toward the bathroom and leaned against the wall facing Mom. She hadn't moved off the edge of the bed.

"He might just be acting like a teenager, you know." He spoke much more quietly then. "Doesn't mean anything."

Mom shrugged him off.

"It could even be something at school. Something from that incident yesterday with Kevin."

"He's had those before," Mom said, "never reacted like this." She looked up at him. "I just hope he doesn't lash out again. Can you imagine what he would be capable of?"

"He won't. Not like that. Even he doesn't know what he can do."

She turned away again.

"It could be something with that girl he's got a crush on, whatsername."

"Evelyn."

"Yeah. Maybe he thinks she doesn't like him, or likes someone else. Guys do crazy things for girls all the time."

"I don't think so," Mom said. She reached across her chest to rub her shoulder.

"Or it could just be a natural part of growing up. Doesn't mean anything more."

"I'm not sure we can risk that," Mom said. "Not with him."

"Well, we can't force him to open up. That would guarantee that he pulls away. The last thing we'd want is any sort of rebellion on our hands, normal teenager type or otherwise."

"We've done such a good job with him," Mom said. "He's a good student. He doesn't misbehave anymore, hasn't for years. He's exactly where he needs to be."

"He is." Dad nodded. "And most of that is because we haven't forced any of our own ideas on him. Remember what Choi said: hint, repetition, give him the basis of an idea so he can form it himself. The way he reacted to Andre tonight, that was great."

Mom sighed. "Poor Andre. I can't imagine how he's going to feel once Odin moves on."

"We'll deal with that when it comes," Dad said. He stepped to the side of the bed and kneeled down in front of Mom. "We've come too far to blow this. Just a couple more years and he'll be ready."

She nodded understanding.

"It might be time to give him a bit more freedom, so he doesn't feel like we're smothering him."

"I just wanted to spend some time with my son, Ben. Try to connect somehow. That's all."

"I don't mean that. I mean we *are* pretty protective of him compared to most kids his age. We say protective, he or they might say strict. It might be time to ease up a little."

"Like what? Get his nose pierced? Take him for a tattoo?"

Dad laughed. "Well, a lot of kids his age are doing that. Hell, I went through my entire senior year high as a kite. Spent most of college that way too."

She tilted her head at him.

"I'm kidding."

"This isn't the time to try to be funny."

He placed a hand on her knee.

"What're most of his friends doing?" she asked.

"I imagine they're doing what high school boys spend most of their time doing: trying to get laid."

"I don't think we can help him with that."

"Not in ways either of us would be comfortable with."

She went quiet.

"You know his friends are all over Facebook and Twitter and whatever else there is," he said. "Instaface. Twitbook," he interjected. Still no laugh. "We've kept him off. Wiggins reported that they rag on him for not texting and not being on any of these things that everyone else is on. Maybe that's something we can do. Make him feel more like he's gaining some kind of freedom. We can track everything he does on them anyway."

"You know I hate that."

"I'm not talking about cameras or microphones. I

mean keeping track of whom he talks to and when. Hell, the desk jockeys at NSA are already doing that to all of us."

"And you know I hate that too."

"Has to be done." He sat down.

"Kids his age shouldn't be on those sites."

"And kids his age shouldn't be smoking crack and getting pregnant and shooting each other, but they are. If allowing our son to send electronic messages to strangers is our greatest concern, then I think we're lucky for that."

"It's not the strangers I'm worried about."

"Greater access is a risk but it's far riskier to keep limiting him like this. If he feels manipulated, he's a lot more likely to pull away."

She nodded absently. Dad took one of her hands as he stood up in front of her. She followed his face with her eyes.

"You're doing great," he said. He leaned down to kiss her forehead. "Only a little while more until he's ready."

The ceiling is a uniform black over my bed. I give my eyes a moment to adjust before looking around the room at the familiar shapes surrounding me. The things I know even when completely blind.

They knew about the incident with Kevin. They mentioned Evelyn by name. Move on, they said. A little while more until he's ready.

"What do they want?" I ask the darkness.

They want what people always want from anything new or unique.

I think for a second. He obviously means they want to use me for their own gain, whoever "they" are.

Any new technology, science, or discovery.

I wait for the answer I know is coming.

A weapon.

He always knocks once before speaking. "Hey," Dad says, "can I come in?"

"One minute," I say, lowering my physics book

to the floor and opening my calc book on the desk. Dad's outside my door in his old Diabetes Fun Run shirt from six years ago and the faded green shorts he's probably owned longer than I've been alive.

"What's up?" I ask.

"We're heading out to get some lunch if you wanna come along."

"Nah," I say, "I'm fine here."

"Have it your way. More tacos for us." He starts to walk away. I begin to close the door. "Oh," he says, stopping and turning back. "One more thing. Remember that conversation we had a couple weeks ago about how all your friends use Facegram and Tweeter?" He purposefully gets the names wrong; it's meant to be casual and disarming. "Mom and I were thinking that with the year ending you should be able to talk with your friends however you please, on the computer, on the phone, CB radio, singing telegram, cup and string. So if you haven't already started secret accounts against our expressed wishes—and you haven't, have you?"

"No."

"Well, you can now but without the secrecy. Just don't go too hard on the texting. If you go over our data limit, I'm paying for it with your college fund. After a year there may not be much left."

"I got it."

"And you're sure about the tacos?" He points in the way a game show host does to an answering contestant.

"I'm sure."

"All right," he says as he starts away again, "have fun being a shut-in."

"I will." I close the door behind him. I sit down at my desk and stare at the open book in front of me, one of the two I'd been flipping open and rotating a couple of minutes earlier. I turn the pages for a couple more minutes without thinking, my fingers twitching like a nervous tick. It was exactly what they'd spoken about last night. Allowing me more freedom, making me think it was my idea. He even delivered the news in the light and fun way that I'd always enjoyed about him. It was so precisely what I pictured. I close my eyes and let my head droop.

They left less than a minute ago. Mom was standing at the end of the hall when Dad turned away from my door. He put his fists up like a boxer, then shrugged. She shook her head and started toward the door.

"All right," Dad said to Andre, who was sitting on the couch. "Let's go."

"What about Odin?" Andre asked.

"He's being moody." He ushered Andre out the front. "Hey, I ever tell you about the tacos I had in Tijuana?" he said as the door closed behind him.

I fling the calculus book across the room. It hits the door and the wood creaks. I launch the physics book as well. Its corner leaves a small dent next to the doorknob. Both books drop to the floor messily.

I'd had the last couple of days to imagine the possibility, not everything it implied, but at least the basic idea of it. The reality is still crushing. The lies, the betrayal of it all. How much of what I knew of my parents, my life, was real and how much was an elaborate ruse made to condition me for some . . . I don't even know yet! I can. I could know everything. But I still can't get myself to do it. Looking into their lives still feels like betrayal. A betrayal of the betrayer, but a betrayal nonetheless. Then I'd be no better than them. Even with all their lies.

My teeth clench. Jaws flex. My hands are wound into tight fists. The pages of my expensive textbooks are bent and folded under themselves. They could have been torn. They still could be.

"Everything," I growl. "Everything they've told me."

Everything.

My hands twitch. "I can't believe it."

Not a word.

"There's got to be some kind of explanation. Some reason."

I have already explained it to you. They want to use you.

I shake my head, feeling myself calming. Logic

taking over. "That can't be all there is. Maybe if I just ask them about it—"

No. You cannot tell them what you know.

His reason is obvious before he says it.

If they know they are compromised, they will react. They will put you somewhere secure and say it is for your own good. Better to leave things as is until the correct opportunity presents itself.

"And what is this correct opportunity?" I say as though a bad taste were lingering in my mouth.

You will know it when it comes. If you do not, I will tell you.

That's exactly what I was afraid of. Wendell being right, having to depend on him, my parents being false, my school, my friends, everything, exactly what I was afraid of. I swipe one hand and smash the physics book against the wall between my room and the kitchen. It hits so hard that I can hear the plates rattle in the cupboards outside. The echo fills the room.

9

I CAN COUNT THE NUMBER OF PEOPLE I'VE SPOKEN TO this week on my fingers. Those few were never beyond monosyllabic utterances: "Yeah," "Fine," "Sure." I haven't even eaten lunch in the usual spot since the issue with David last Friday. There's just nothing to say. Not to them. Not to my parents. Actually, there's plenty to say to all of them, but nothing that would do any good. Every time I see them, Mom and Dad I mean, in the morning before school, during the ride here with Mom, arriving home after school to see her again, at dinner, it takes all my control not to stick a knife in their faces and demand answers. Although at

dinner it would probably be a butter knife. Wendell is right, best to lay low for a while. I know I'm
acting strangely. I can't help it. It took them only
a couple of days to adjust. They probably think
this is a phase, something that will fade quickly.
It's not, not really, at least. For all I know, this is
life now. This is how we'll communicate until the
"correct opportunity presents itself." Whatever
that means.

Dad's still calls me "shut-in" on the "rare occa-
sion" when I "make an appearance" outside of my
room. I've barely even spoken to Wendell beyond
practicing with manipulating objects in new ways.
He talks. I don't. Last night was the first time I
managed to get three books in the air at the same
time, even opened two of them before the third
started to fall. It's pretty intense, holding a consis-
tent picture in my mind. Not allowing my attention
to waver or the mental image to change. That's the
key. It doesn't sound difficult, imagining what you
want to see, but it's hard to keep focused on that

among all the surrounding distractions, especially since I'm so accustomed to multi-tasking. It gets a lot harder to add things like motion, manipulation, and multiple objects to that picture. After several days of practice, I managed to get two corners of my bed to lift smoothly. It's a start.

Usually before classes begin, I sit with Brent and all of them on the benches near the front entrance, just outside the windows. That's where a lot of the junior boys hang out, always been that way. Next year we'll move up to the senior benches near the hallway entrance inside the main building. This is how we've been conditioned. The interior "senior" benches are considered better because the wind doesn't push the rain and snow under the roof, forcing everyone to consolidate on the two benches against the wall. The seniors even have a good view of us juniors through the tinted glass. We can see them exaggeratedly pointing and laughing while we scrambled to keep our stuff dry and try to pile a dozen people onto two benches meant to fit three or four apiece.

Better for them is when the girls come by. I remember talking with Tyler once, a senior in my Euro class, when Jenny Robinson stopped at the benches to talk with Brent. She bent back against the wall, probably not remembering that it's glass, and her skirt slowly started to ride up, showing the underwear covering half of one butt cheek. From what I've heard of her, she might've done that on purpose. All the guys on the benches leaned forward trying to get as low as possible before one of the teachers or security guards caught them. I glanced at her ass once and made an effort not to look back again. It was pretty nice, but I didn't want to be like the rest of the guys. One of them laid on the floor with his feet on the bench. Another made smacking motions and waggled his tongue. They looked like salivating dogs begging for scraps, each more pathetic than the next. None of the juniors had that view. Another perk of being a senior.

But that's next year, for now I've taken to walking straight through the entrance and directly to my first class of the day, no matter what's up in the daily rotation. I pass the juniors outside and the seniors inside, the janitors sweeping the front, the teachers eating breakfast in their classes. I plunk my bag against the wall next to me and sit with my knees bent and elbows folded across them. I never catch anyone staring as they pass, but I know at least one person is. Someone here is watching me. Just like at home. The difference is that at home I know who's watching. I'm not sure if that makes it better or worse.

Today it's British Literature back in the Reading for Dumbasses Room 228. The same room where I had my last conversation where I said more than fifteen words. Brit Lit is one of the few classes I actually have to make a bit of an effort in because, unlike the others, there aren't concrete answers to most questions. It's still not hard. Just choose a thesis statement and find support from the book, or better yet, the previous classes. I typically ace papers by paraphrasing Mr. Romero's own words. Guy loves everything he says, even when he got half of it from Mrs. Wilson before she retired six years ago or from the preface of some special edition of the book. If a student quotes other people without giving credit it's plagiarism; if the teacher does it it's education. That's fair.

"Hey, Odin."

I look up to see Evelyn standing a few feet from me. She's leaned to the side with her binder held in both hands in front of her waist. Her dark hair hangs like a cascade over her shoulder and around her arm. Her silver bracelet charms swing slightly, two little hearts and one skull. I try not to stare at the firm legs running from the bottom of her skirt to the top of her boots. I don't want to be one of the begging dogs.

"Umm," I say, ever so suavely, "hi."

"You okay?"

"Yeah. I'm fine."

She straightens up. "You just seem really quiet lately. Brent was even asking yesterday if I knew anything about it."

I take a second to think. "Just not a lot to talk about lately, I guess."

"Is it that stuff with Kevin?" I shake my head. "He's just a jerk. You can't let that bother you."

"That's not it. Not really."

"People will always find a reason to talk about anyone. I mean, remember last year when everyone said Nicole was pregnant because she had the stomach flu for a week?" She laughs lightly, happily. "It's like that old game telephone. It's all hearsay. You can't trust any of it." A bell rings in my head. "They hear only part of the story and then embellish because real life is boring." She smiles. It makes me smile too. "You can't let it bother you."

"I know. It still does."

"Those who actually saw it know exactly what happened. Oh, do you mind talking?" I shake my head. "Good." She moves around to my side, only a couple of feet between us. She puts her binder and bag down and presses her skirt against her as she sits. She's classy like that, not like Jenny Robinson. "Kevin was just being a dick. You know he's like that."

"Yeah."

"To be honest, part of me wanted to see you knock him out." Her head tilts down with her eyes up. Her cheeks pull back into a crooked grin. A sort of evil-cute look that's just perfect. Skulls and hearts. Subtle, and that's one of the things I like about her. Cross country athlete and theatre geek. There's a way she seems to play with people's expectations. Not in a malicious way, in more of an amused one. Amused when she knows something other people don't. I understand that feeling. "I mean, I don't want anyone to get hurt," she says, "but he's just such an asshole sometimes. It'd be nice to see him . . . humbled, I guess."

"Yeah," I chuckle, "that sounds right."

"It's all such an act too," she says, "he wasn't like that in freshman year at all. He was actually pretty nice."

I furrow my brow at her. "Really?"

"Yeah. Mostly nice, I guess. He was even kinda sweet." I feel an urge to make Kevin swallow his own teeth. "Not anymore. It's like he's trying to be something he's not because he's scared of being what he is. Or I dunno, something like that. Or maybe the nice part was the act and he's really just an asshole."

"More likely," I say.

"I guess it's like, if you pretend to be a jerk for long enough you're not pretending anymore, you know?" The hall lights reflect in her eyes like ridges on a seashell.

"Totally," I say.

"Yeah," she says, "I figured you would understand what I mean." She looks into the hallway as another student enters the class room across from us. It's only now that I notice several others are walking past. "Humbled is a good thing."

A few other students pass. One turns quickly as I look at him.

"Like you did with David," she says.

"You heard about that?"

"Of course! I mean," her voice goes quieter, "people were already being idiots about the thing with Kevin, so the thing with David just added to it." She speaks even more quietly, requiring me to tilt my head nearer to hers. We're separated by only a few inches. Her hair smells like lavender shampoo. "Did he really get his cousin pregnant?"

"What?" I laugh. She sways back. "No," I say, "I was messing with him."

"I thought so." She shows her crooked grin. "Another rumor, right?"

"Yeah."

"I'd believe that with him, though." She leans in and lowers her tone again. Faces me although her eyes dart around the hall next to us. "We had to share a practice field with the baseball team once and he just stood there staring at us the whole time we were stretching. It made everyone uncomfortable."

I nod. Another salivating dog. Another predator.

I don't want anyone to feel like they have to be cautious around me.

"I don't know why you and Brent hang out with that guy."

I shrug. "He's okay most of the time. Harmless, more or less."

"Oh, yeah," she perks up quickly, her hand almost brushing my arm. "Is your party still happening?"

I blink rapidly a few times. It's been planned for tomorrow night at the Bowl-O-Drome. I haven't even thought about it for a week.

"I mean, that hasn't changed, right? I've been meaning to ask but you've seemed a bit . . . unapproachable lately."

"Sorry," I say, "but yeah, still on."

"Because I got you this great present and I'd hate for it to go to waste."

Condoms, I wanna ask, but of course I don't.

"No, I mean, as far as I know it's happening. I didn't really organize it, though."

"You know how many people are coming?"

I shake my head. "Brent, Richard, David I suppose, unfortunately, most of the bowling team and a few other guys, I think."

"You invite any other girls?"

"A couple from the girls' team, Merlinda and Terri, I think they'll be there."

"Okay," she says, nodding, "not too many. Good." She turns back to face me. "I just hate those kinds of parties where you go for the person and then never get to hang out with that person because there are so many other people there, you know?"

"You can hang out with me all you like."

She smiles widely. "Cool. Anything else I should bring?"

"No," I say. Just yourself, I don't say.

"All right, just Maria and the super awesome gift that I'm totally not overselling." One of her cheeks pulls back into the crooked smile once again. She hadn't done that so much before now. Could be that she's getting more comfortable with showing that side of herself. Could be something else.

The hall around us is now loud with lockers slamming, footsteps, and students walking into classrooms. Evelyn looks around for a moment. I do the same, catching a couple of quick turn-aways.

"You ready for the physics exam today?"

"Right," I say, "that's today."

"Oh, I'm sure you'll ace it like you always do."

"I haven't been studying much."

"That's what you always say before getting another, like, ninety-five on the exam. I wish it was that easy for me."

"I'm sure you'll do great too."

"Yeah, but I have to work for it." She brings her knees in and starts to stand up. I put my hand on the ground to push myself up after her.

"We could share notes after class," I say, "like, compare answers. Try to guess how we did."

"Sure," she says, tilting her head to let her hair

fall. She brings her binder back in front of her waist. "I can find out how many I got wrong."

"You'll be fine."

"Thanks." She looks around, then at her sporty pink-and-black watch. "Anyway, glad to hear you're doing okay. Don't let any of this stuff bother you. It's all just an act anyway."

"Yeah," I say, not really nodding and not really at her.

"Talk to ya later," she says as she steps into the hallway traffic. I watch her leave before entering the classroom and walking to my seat.

An act. She doesn't know the half. Unless . . .

Shit.

Mom and Dad even mentioned Evelyn by name. And that hearsay comment . . . she'd be the perfect one to say that. The perfect one to get me to talk after a week of silence. How would Mom and Dad know about Evelyn unless they had someone here? Wiggins, that was the name. I don't know anyone named that. How would whoever this Wiggins is know that I like Evelyn unless . . . Someone else I know. A teacher or a student. A spy.

It can't be her, though. I know her well enough. She's not *that* good of an actress. But it would be easy to find out. See if she's ever spoken with either of my parents.

At the front of the room, Romero says something about James Joyce.

No matter. I could learn everything I'd ever need to know about every person here. Who's lying and who isn't. Evelyn, she's always been off-limits like that. Her especially. I don't even want to imagine what it would mean if she's been a part of my parent's "Department" this entire time. Using that sly smile to lure me in. Can't this one thing be honest? Everything else can be a lie but this, whatever it is. I'm not sure what I'd do without that one little shred of hope. Let at least this lone thing in my life be true. There's a reason people keep certain things private. The illusion is better.

10

I HURRY OUT OF CLASS FOR ONCE. PARTLY TO AVOID unnecessary talk, but mostly to be at the junior benches outside when Evelyn walks by on her way to her bus stop. I take a seat on the bench facing the walkway, not the door, so I won't appear eager. I casually drop my bag in front of me. I'll see her tomorrow at the party but it'd be nice to talk a bit before then too. It's been the only part of my week worth remembering. The only part that I actually care about keeping. Besides, if in some completely unlikely, outlandish scenario, Evelyn were actually being used to pull me back into "their" control, I should at least enjoy the company.

I watch as other students file out of the building in their groups. Everyone is happier, their expressions louder and their gestures bigger than on any other day of the week. Right after classes end on Friday is the longest time from when classes begin again. Not including anomalies like vacations and holidays, of course. Every second brings more of the same closer.

I crane my neck over and around the other students, walking or sitting, looking for Evelyn or Maria or some other member of their group. I look through the dark glass as best I can to see if they're coming. I keep my arms folded and elbows on my knees, positioned to look nonchalant as soon as they appear. The benches are now almost full except for mine. I'm the only one sitting here, on the last third of the bench, bag at my feet. The others all have three or four seated. I know why. I no longer care.

In fact, if it weren't for being stuck in the same place for four years, I wouldn't know any of the people sitting at these benches or coming out of this building. Once our time here is up, I'll probably never see or speak to these people again. I might stay in touch with some friends, Brent most likely, possibly Richard, if they're not complete frauds. Hopefully Evelyn will remain close, *very* close, and of her own free will and not some kind of scheme. But other than that, I don't really care. So what if they talk?

I feel a scowl forming on my face as I survey the students in the area. I shake it off to check for Evelyn or her group again. Still nothing. Meanwhile those around me are busy talking quietly among themselves, with only a few occasionally glancing in my direction. Watching. Always watching. Never interacting. The bench remains unoccupied.

Their whispers and stares and quick look-aways have absolutely no power over me. They have no idea who I am or what I can do. Not even this Wiggins character does. I am unique. I am better. Whether they know it or not.

"Look at that," I hear just over the rest of the chatter, "all alone."

I see Kevin approaching the benches. He wears a brand new shirt with the right amount of fading and chipped print to make it look old. Dylan and Eric accompany him, his old cronies. Then T.J. and Ross, a couple of new additions to their group after Adam, the guy who was with Kevin the day on the basketball court, ditched them when he started dating Isabel from the Spanish Club.

I stare through the glass like I'm not listening.

"Look at that," Kevin continues, "even his friends don't like him."

I glance over quickly and immediately regret it as my eyes catch with his. I look away on instinct. The same quick eye movement I've been seeing all week. It means I'm aware of them. I've engaged. I hear and will need to respond somehow.

"Loser," says Eric.

"That weird, nerdy kind nobody likes. Has to make up his own friends."

I keep my eyes ahead and fight every urge to stare him down. I feel the familiar pressure of my jaw tensing. Many of the other conversations have slowed or quieted. Those who have stopped talking now stare openly.

"A weird loser that nobody likes who's obsessed with a chick who'll fuck anyone but him."

Dylan lets out an "Ooooooh," followed by another comment of "Burn." Control. It takes all I have not to rush at Kevin, push him to the ground, and slam his head into the concrete until he stops moving. Control.

He only does this because you allow it.

My eyes close. I feel my chest rise and fall with every breath.

"What's the matter, Oddin? No teachers around to run to? Pussy." Eric laughs. The crowd surrounding us has stopped talking. No more quick turns. Every eye is on me.

He has power over you.

"Just the weird kid that nobody likes."

My fingers are shaking.

You can make him stop.

"Has to make up his own friends."

"Such a loser," Dylan says. The others laugh.

Right now.

"The fuck is your problem?" I say, loudly. I stare directly into Kevin's eyes, the irises barely visible through the glare off his glasses.

"What?" Kevin asks.

"What's the matter?" I say. Beyond him I catch a glimpse of a button nose and round cheeks. "You need fake hearing aids to go with your fake ass glasses?" He stares back at me, looking as though even he can't believe what's happening. I try my best to flex my jaw between sentences. Narrow my eyes. A lion, as Wendell said, staring down prey. "Or maybe all the bullshit running from your mouth is clogging your ears."

He looks at those around him as though trying to scoff, but I see nervousness in the way he shifts his weight from one foot to the other. His feet point away from me.

"Fell into any staircases lately?"

He's the only one who will understand that. It rattles him. I can see his pant leg swaying. Eric slaps him on the shoulder before gesturing at me.

"You gonna take this?"

"Fuck you, Oddin."

I shrug as casually as possible.

The entire world has gone quiet. There is nothing happening but this. Kevin looks at the students gathered in a circle around us. I catch Evelyn again, slowing her stride, peeking over a few others. Maria is next to her, very clearly watching. Kevin takes a step toward me.

"At least I don't hear voices."

The stooges chuckle.

"Ha! Such a loser," says Eric.

"Yeah, such a loser," says Dylan.

Kevin takes another step.

Time to end the chaos.

I stand up, trying my best not to visibly shake.

"How about I kick your ass again?" Kevin looks at everyone but me. "Right in front of everybody."

There may be fewer than thirty gathered, but the crowd feels impossibly large.

I picture the bag on the bench behind me. The twenty pounds of books inside. I see Evelyn peeking over some boy's shoulder. Kevin sees me looking and peeks over as well. Evelyn looks away. She said she wanted to see him humbled.

There must be order.

"You know," he says, leaning his face closer to mine. His breath is minty. A stick of gum after lunch every day. As though a better smell will improve the shit pouring out of his mouth. "Why don't you ask your dream girl what my dick tastes like?"

Show them.

My fingers twitch at my side. I picture the bag floating an inch in the air.

"How much she loved sucking me off."

My lips pull back. I snarl at him.

"Me and the whole track team."

I know that isn't true, but knowing doesn't help.

"Everyone except you."

I roar. I fling my arm around. My bag rams into Kevin's face. His glasses snap. His bones crunch. A twenty pound bag flying three feet at fifty miles an hour directly into his head. More than two hundred twenty joules. Stronger than gravity. Like being hit with the heaviest bowling ball, only heavier, right in the skull. He'll be lucky if it doesn't crack. Headshot.

I hear the rush of breath all around.

He's down, flat on his back, quiet and still. Eyes shut. A trickle of blood rolls along his upper lip with another above his eye. He's breathing. That's a relief, but it also sucks. I think about picking the bag up and smacking him with it again. Again and again. Until he's nothing but pulp on the concrete.

The entire world remains quiet.

I look up at his stooges and the shocked faces around them. I hope I look like a lion. I hope I look like a king. Blood pours out of Kevin's nose and eye, dripping onto the concrete. His jaw is red and beginning to swell. His big, nerd frames have snapped in half. One plastic lens is cracked almost entirely through. I pick up my backpack, checking the bottom for any blood or dirt.

I glare at the crowd one more time. Their eyes are wide, mouths open. They look like they haven't breathed for days. I keep my bag hanging from one arm, it's heavy but I don't show it. I take one more look at Kevin, the blood now rolling off his face and onto the concrete. I sweep one of his fake lenses with my foot and step over him. Evelyn is just barely in view. Her eyes are down. Her hands over her mouth. I hate that she saw this. I also love it. She got to see Kevin humbled. And I got to be the one who humbled him.

I feel their eyes following as I walk, the force of the backpack pulling on the same arm I used to convert it from container to weapon. Their whispers begin, grow louder as I continue on, become whispers again. I don't look back. Not once. There is no reason. The reaction is not always equal. It doesn't matter.

At the bus stop, with no one else around, I let my bag drop to my feet. I breathe out deeply. I close my eyes.

He was the first.

My chest and shoulders rise as I breathe again. I feel the air pushing my body up, every atom, molecule, particle around me.

You will show them order.

I open my eyes. The grass and trees, the sky, the road, the houses, the bus stop sign, every color is sharper, more vibrant. They pop against each other.

You will make them learn.

My jaw aches. My hands have stopped shaking. The few cars that pass probably don't even notice me. I stand completely still. All potential energy. Nothing in motion.

Now we can start.

I let myself drop onto the bus stop bench. My eyes close again. There's water under my eyelids. I inhale deep and feel one tear form.

What have I done?

11

I MAKE SURE TO LEAVE THE FIVE PIN STANDING. IT breaks my closed streak: strike, strike, strike, nine spare, strike, eight spare, strike. Only eight frames into the second game and I'm already twenty over my full game average. The spares are where the ball started too far off line to push before it was out of my reach. If I punch out, which I probably will, it'll be my highest score ever, even higher than the last game, which was my previous highest score ever.

Why did you do that?

There's a wide buffer between me and the closest person in the alley, the four lanes which I

195

reserved for my party. I'm the only one here. The remaining sixteen lanes have groups of people at them, bowling, talking, eating, having a great little time. There's the crowd at the video game center, the middle school kids who've never picked up a bowling ball but can kick your ass at any fighting game you choose. A group at the front desk is asking about open lanes. Then there's me, in my wide bubble. Just me and the voice in my head.

"I don't want the attention," I say quietly, staring at the ball return for my blue-green fifteen-pounder.

Such a waste.

I wiggle my fingers over the hand drier.

You could be remarkable. Instead you decide to settle.

I close my eyes and the images come back to me. Kevin, on the ground, blood gushing from two places, his nose and eye smashed, jaw like he's chewing a golf ball. I keep expecting for his parents or the police to come looking for me. Instead, there was silence.

Why?

"Why what?" I say, as my ball appears from the covered shoot of the return. I scoop it up with both hands.

Why settle for mediocre when you can have greatness?

I place my fingers in the ball, take my mark on the second line, and cock my elbow back. I enter my usual stance, bend my knees slightly, lean forward, the familiar motion of left foot first, right, left, begin arm swing, right, left, release, follow through. The ball hits three feet down the lane and slightly off-line from the head pin. I picture the ball straightening out. It hits the pocket clean. The pins scatter in every direction. Strike.

See? See how easy it is?

I turn away as the pin reset falls. "Maybe I don't want greatness. Maybe I just want to be normal again."

That is not possible. Not anymore.

"I wish it was."

An alley attendant starts to approach my empty lanes. I look down at the ball return, hoping he'll leave me alone.

"Excuse me."

Dammit. I look up at him.

"I know you've reserved these, but it's been an hour. There are other people waiting . . . "

I look back at the ball return.

"We're wondering if they could use these to play."

I wiggle my fingers at the drier again. It's all part of the routine.

"Or if you know when your party may arrive."

"Go ahead," I say, watching as my ball appears. "They're not coming."

I woke up this morning to the chirp of my cell phone. It took a moment to remember where I was before the previous day rushed back to mind. I'd gone directly home, to my room, eaten dinner without speaking more than five words, and straight to bed. I slept through the whole night without waking once. I can't remember the last time that happened. I answered the phone just before the voicemail clicked on.

"Hey man," said Brent after my greeting, "happy birthday!"

"Thanks," I replied, hearing the sleep still in my voice. "You're the first to say that so far."

"You just wake up?"

"Yeah, long week, you know?"

"I can imagine." I'm sure he can't. "Anyway, I'm really sorry but I can't make to the party tonight. My grandma had a bad fall last night and the whole family had to stay in the hospital with her. Mom's making me go back again today." It was a lie, he spent last night gaming online with David. They talked a lot about me.

"That sucks. I hope she's okay," I say, trying to sound empathetic.

"Anyway, sorry for missing it, since the party

was, like, my idea and everything. I'd totally be there if I could."

"I know."

"I'll give you your present on Monday, cool?"

"Sure."

"All right, gotta go. Happy birthday."

"Thanks."

He hung up.

I bounded off my bed and toward the computer on the desk to check my email. There were eleven unread messages: Teddy and Lucas, guys from the bowling team who eat lunch with us, Merlinda and Terri, the only girls I invited other than Evelyn, Mike, Pierce, Richard, a couple others from classes and stuff. They were all sent late last night, all with some mention of birthday in the subject—*Happy Birthday!, Your birthday party, HBD*—and all saying that some last minute thing came up—illness, sudden exam, surprise term paper, grounded, dead cat . . . Seriously Terri? dead cat? That's so easy to check . . . And another sick grandma—not one mentioned the real reason why they didn't want to come. I'm dangerous. I'm a freak. A menace. A demon. I am everything they say I am. There's no point trying to deny or explain; that would only make me a liar as well.

For all the tough talk about beating anyone who steps to them, or pounding the shit out of kids they don't like, or knifings and headshots, the brutality of even the smallest confrontation freaks everyone the hell out. Of course, it probably wasn't a small confrontation at all.

After several hours to spread from student to student, with each one adding their own twists and embellishments, I probably threw him across twelve feet of concrete, while floating, glowing red, and speaking in tongues. I continued to beat him on the ground, snarling and challenging everyone to try to stop me. I summoned a fireball into my palm or a meteor from the heavens.

The broken nose was obvious, probably the jaw too. By this morning, twenty hours later, Kevin probably has a broken eye socket. Or a completely smashed-in face. A fractured skull. He got a concussion. Permanent brain damage. He's in the hospital. In a coma.

In reality, his friends helped him back into one of the boys' bathrooms. He washed his face and waited in there for the spectators to leave. Eric drove him home in his car and told his parents Kevin had an accident while riding a friend's bike around the school. Brakes went out and crashed badly into a wall. He did go to the hospital to get his nose fixed, some stitches, and his jaw wired. He has an appointment next week to be re-evaluated and have his stitches removed.

In the rumor, he was carried off to the school's health room, taken to the hospital, rolled through emergency on a stretcher, and is receiving food through a tube in his arm. All because I psychically lifted him up and drove his head directly into the concrete a dozen times and then breathed fire into the air.

And, of course, no one will ask if any of this is true because I'd only deny it, which would mean it's all true, and I can't be trusted anyway, because I'm dangerous and a freak and a demon and everything else the rumor says.

Dad broke this Mobius strip of thought with a single knock on my door. "Hey, Odin," he said, "you awake yet?"

"Yeah."

"Well, you wanna come out here? There are people ready to celebrate you being born."

" . . . In a little while. I'm sorting out some party plans for tonight."

"Okay. Don't take too long, though. The candles might burn the house down."

" . . . You're having cake already?"

"No. I mean that maybe we'll decide to light candles and maybe they'll burn the house down. Just so you'll be ready in case that happens."

I could picture the little smile on his face. The mockery of it. He's always so clever.

Good.

"What?" I said quietly, hoping Dad had already walked away.

Fewer distractions.

"You mean fewer things to help me ignore you." Wendell had been silent most of the night and morning, but I'd also gotten better at tuning him out.

Fewer people to lie to you. To pull you away from what you should do.

"I have no idea what that is anymore."

Fewer peons keeping you from becoming a ruler.

"But without the peons there is no ruler."

There was the now familiar tingle through my mind.

A true ruler will make people follow. He creates a world where they have no choice.

"That sounds awful," I said, sitting back at my desk. I deleted each of the excuse emails without replying. No reply would help anyway.

It is the only escape from chaos.

"Whatever. I don't care anymore."

Not now, but one day you will.

My phone beeped with a text message. Only one person does that.

Happy birthday! the text read, with a big smiley face after the exclamation. *Hope you're having a wonderful morning* with a bright sun. I knew what was coming next. *Maria can't come tonight and my mom says I can't go without her. Really really sorry,* followed by a sad, crying face. *Hope you still have a great time!* The messages ended with a little cartoon cake.

I felt like crushing the phone in my hand, if I could do that, or at least throwing it to the ground. Then I'd toss my computer against the wall, fling the desk over, probably scream a few times, smash my chair through the window, and light the whole place on fire. I could blame it on the candles. Of course I did none of that. I'm not stupid. And I'm not dangerous. I have control. Instead, I closed my eyes, took a breath, and started typing back.

That sucks, I wrote, trying to be as normal as possible. She was the only person I'd heard from who was there yesterday. If even she wasn't going to mention what happened, then I wouldn't either. *Won't be as much fun without you.* I hit send and wait. At least her excuse was believable.

They only stand in your way.

A minute later comes the reply. *Awww. I'm really sorry. But it's still your birthday. Have fun!* Another big smiley. I doubted that she was actually smiling.

Maybe just a quick drop by? I'd love to see you, I wrote, knowing she wouldn't do that and there wouldn't be a party. That might be better, give me a chance to explain. She and I always communicate best when alone. I erased the message and wrote, *Maybe just drop by with the awesome present you totally didn't oversell.* I sent and waited again.

Let them go.

I close the tenth frame with a pair of strikes. Extra shot coming. If I punch out, which I will, I'll have a new high of a two hundred twenty-seven. I'm still waiting for her to reply.

***

I tried crying. Really, I actually *tried* to cry. Nothing happened. I wasn't particularly sad. I wasn't even particularly angry. After a full evening, night, and morning, there wasn't much emotion left. I had no idea what would happen next but, for some odd reason, I didn't fear it. Sure, dozens of my classmates saw me lift a bag with my mind and launch it into another student's head. I could still be called into the principal's office for fighting or the police station for assault. My friends abandoned me on the one day of the year when they'd usually do whatever I ask. My parents are probably spies set up to watch my every move for some mysterious agency. I've pretty much blown my chances with the only girl I've really wanted to spend time with. And a voice is my head is telling me to do things. But, there is freedom in knowing you're completely screwed. You don't have to give a shit anymore. What else can happen? I put my phone in my pocket and step outside.

"There he is!" Mom said.

"Finally," Andre said, sitting on the couch. He clutched his stomach overdramatically. "I'm starving."

"There's my birthday boy," Mom said in that tone that I never wanted her to use in public, back when I gave a shit. She gave me a kiss on the cheek and a big hug. I put one arm around to pat her on the back. "C'mon, you can do better than that." I rolled my eyes. "Fine," she said, moving away. "But I'm happy for you anyway."

"Dying of starvation," said Andre, flopping around on the couch.

"He's fussy because I said we weren't having breakfast until you came out," Mom said quietly.

"I'm making French toast. And you are eating some."

I shrugged.

"He finally emerges from his cave," Dad said exiting my parents' room at the front of the house. He walked through the living room with a big smile. He stopped in front of me, nodded, and put his hand out to shake. "Congratulations," he said. "Not really a kid anymore but still young enough to force into cheap household labor."

"Awesome," I said.

"Indeed it is."

I began moving toward the table when I felt Dad's hand grab my shoulder. He pulled me around into a big hug, a reminder that he's still several inches and almost eighty pounds bigger than I am. Honestly, he could probably crush me if given a reason.

"I'm proud of you, son," he said before releasing. "Never forget that."

"I won't."

He nodded again and walked away.

"Finally," he said, seeing Mom cooking. "I'm starving." He glanced back at Andre, looking for acknowledgement of his quote. Andre didn't notice, too busy staring at the pan on the stovetop. It must be so tough when your brilliance goes unnoticed.

"What time are you meeting your friends?" Mom asked without turning from the pan.

"We're meeting at the Bowl-O-Drome at five thirty. But most people probably won't be there until six." Even by then I'd already given up all hope of anyone other than myself showing up, but saying anything about it would prompt questions whose answers would only prompt more questions with even worse answers. Like Dad says, there's a reason people keep certain things private. It's because they don't want to hurt us. Yeah, I'm sure that's the only reason.

As far as I know, they haven't heard anything about the incidents with Kevin, the return of

Wendell, or all the practice I've been putting into these . . . I guess they could be called powers. As long as I keep it all to myself, never let on, never deviate from the conditioning, they shouldn't suspect a thing. Brent's parents don't know about the bullet he carries, Richard's parents don't know about the occasional joint, David's parents don't about the thing with his cousin's picture. David never called or emailed. Didn't expect him to. Still, no reason for my parents to suspect anything has changed unless I give them one. I can be careful about it. I'm smarter than they are. I'm smarter than all of them.

I begin the third game with a five-bagger. As long as the ball hits between the third and fourth arrows on the right, I can adjust the angle toward the pocket even halfway down the lane. I imagine how I want the ball to move, the angle, the speed, the curve, and it happens. The pins fly back. Five straight. Halfway to perfection.

Very good.

"I'm getting better."

You are. Becoming impressive.

I continue my routine, everything from wiggling my fingers over the hand drier to releasing on the third left step. The ball strikes the pocket. The pins fly back, ricochet around, and completely miss the seven pin in the left corner. I stare at it, as though looking will make it fall. It can normally be a pretty tough spare. The pinsetter doesn't come down.

I reach to press the pin reset button but . . . why? I look at the rest of the alley around me. The four guys closest are two lanes over and busy drinking and changing each others' names in the scoring computer to "Ass" and "Tits." Why should I have to settle for less than I'm capable of just because they do? They may be unable to roll a perfect game but for me, it's hardly an effort. Isn't it therefore the obligation of those who can achieve to do so?

I turn to face the pin. I imagine it falling over, as though nudged by a breeze. The pin falls.

Wait, it worked? Awesome.

I reach again for the pin reset and notice one of the guys in the other lane looking at me. I say nothing and press the button. The computer records the strike.

You are learning. Finally.

"Learning what?" I say quietly with my head down.

Not to limit yourself.

I wait for my ball, wiggling my fingers at the hand drier.

They have done everything they can to limit you. They have done it so well that you have adopted ways to limit yourself.

I say nothing. He's right. I've done more to get in my own way than anyone else has.

You should never accept limits. Theirs or yours. You are beyond such things.

The machine spits the ball out. I begin the routine, the way I taught myself was the proper way to work. The way I've been conditioned to think was best. The only way I've tried.

I stand straight up, keep the ball curled in my right arm and let my left hand drop. I walk up easily to the line and push the ball out onto the lane. I picture the headpin flying back, the others following it, scattering like an explosion. I picture the pins shattering into a million specks of dust. They shoot off the edge of the lane before the ball even reaches the gutter.

I stand and look up at the score on the screen. I barely hear one of the guys in the nearby lane over the noise of falling pins, talking, and video games. "Holy shit," he says, looking at his buddies, "that kid has a perfect game through seven." I keep my eyes on the scoreboard and smile.

Now that was impressive.

I look down and away, keeping my face hidden. "Best game of my life."

No. What is impressive is that you are finally accepting your place. Finally allowing yourself to reach your potential.

"And what is that exactly?" I say quietly. "You're always talking about all these things I could do but you've never once explained that."

I can offer you a possibility. If you let me.

I don't hesitate. Not anymore. "Show me."

Relax. Think of nothing.

"That's a lot harder than people make it sound."

Do not think. Just do.

I close my eyes, stare at the black, and breathe slowly. It's as though I'm visualizing my next shot. But I visualize nothing. I picture nothing. Breathe out.

Then a window opens in my mind. A single thin shaft of light from the outside rushes to illuminate the dark interior.

I see myself, or someone who looks exactly like

me, standing, no, floating, down a road between a series of small buildings. The vehicles ahead push back as he approaches. His eyes are a glowing white that appears to sizzle. I sense the energy rippling in every direction. I feel the muscles in my mouth move, the exhalation of words, hear my voice in the distance.

"What is this?"

This is you.

His—my—hands turn. Space twists around me.

This is us.